NEVER LOOK BACK

JACK NOBLE
BOOK 16

L.T. RYAN

LIQUID MIND MEDIA

THE JACK NOBLE SERIES

The Recruit (Short Story)
The First Deception (Prequel 1)
Noble Beginnings (Jack Noble #1)
A Deadly Distance (Jack Noble #2)
Ripple Effect (Bear Logan)
Thin Line (Jack Noble #3)
Noble Intentions (Jack Noble #4)
When Dead in Greece (Jack Noble #5)
Noble Retribution (Jack Noble #6)
Noble Betrayal (Jack Noble #7)
Never Go Home (Jack Noble #8)
Beyond Betrayal (Clarissa Abbot)
Noble Judgment (Jack Noble #9)
Never Cry Mercy (Jack Noble #10)
Deadline (Jack Noble #11)
End Game (Jack Noble #12)
Noble Ultimatum (Jack Noble #13)
Noble Legend (Jack Noble #14)

Get your very own Jack Noble merchandise today! Click the link below to find coffee mugs, t-shirts, and even signed copies of your favorite L.T. Ryan thrillers! https://ltryan.ink/EvG_

Receive a free copy of The Recruit. Visit:
https://ltryan.com/jack-noble-newsletter-signup-1

PART 1

CHAPTER 1

THE DUST-COVERED ROAD JUTTED OUT OF THE PACKED EARTH and blocked half of the faded-brown silhouette of Lewistown, Montana. A mile or two stood in front of Jack Noble and a hopeful reunion with Reese McSweeney, a woman he'd fallen in love with twice before. A woman he'd lost twice before. The first time, she'd been taken from him. The second, he from her. This reunion would be more bitter than sweet. The news he brought would tear her soul apart.

Her brother had died.

And it had happened on Noble's watch.

Noble had taken a week to make the drive from Austin, Texas. Partly because he stopped for a couple of days outside of Denver. Partly because the Jeep Wrangler he'd made the trip in decided to make a stop of its own shortly after he'd crossed into Wyoming. He enjoyed the break. The anonymity. The respite from thinking about an upcoming job. While not as dangerous as what he typically faced, it would be one of the hardest conversations he'd ever had.

He pulled off the road and cut the engine a few hundred yards from town. A cloud of dust took its time dissipating in the still air.

During his detour in Douglas, Wyoming, he'd read up on Lewistown. Studied maps and learned the locations of various businesses. There wasn't much to the place. Like most small towns, activity centered on Main Street. The heart of the city spread out ten blocks northwest and southeast of the thoroughfare before giving way to the plains.

He felt the approaching vehicle through his boots before he heard the sound of the old V-8. A primer-gray pickup truck shimmered on the horizon behind him. It advanced quickly, right turn signal flashing as it decelerated until finally pulling off the road and coming to a stop a dozen yards behind Noble's Wrangler, kicking up a fresh cloud of dirt. A longhorn skull was attached to the grill, wrapped in place with barbed wire. The grimy windshield obscured the driver. There was no passenger. The driver's door opened and a pair of brown cowboy boots hit the ground. An older man with a cropped beard and silver hair hanging past his shoulders stepped around the door and walked up to Noble, one hand in his pocket, the other resting on his .357 which he open carried in a worn leather holster that had more cracks in it than the old guy's face.

"Car trouble, friend?" the older man asked.

Noble shook his head. "Taking in the scenery."

The man turned in a semi-circle and back again. He didn't look impressed by the plains behind him, or mountains rising to the west. Majestic, even though they were some fifty miles away.

"To each their own, I suppose," he said. "You ain't from around here."

Noble shook his head, said nothing.

"Where you coming from?"

"South. Texas."

"That where you call home?"

"Don't call any place home at the moment."

"Where'd you used to call home?"

"Florida at one time. More recently, New York, but even that's been a while."

The old guy lifted an eyebrow. "The city?"

Noble shrugged. "It has its benefits."

"Might not think it to look at me, but I lived in Manhattan at one time."

"Get the hell outta here." Noble smiled. "Manhattan, Kansas, right?"

The older man brushed off the suggestion with a sweeping gesture of his hand. "So what all was between New York and here?"

"You ask a lot of questions."

"And you don't like answering them."

"Cop?"

The old man shook his head. "Nothing that exciting." He glanced back at an approaching SUV, stuck out a hand and waved. After the swirling dust settled, he said, "You just passing through our quaint little town?"

"Might stick around for a bit. Do some fishing. Sightseeing."

"Got a *job* to do here?"

Noble paused a beat. Who was this guy? Why'd he phrase it like that? "Of sorts."

"Not selling anything, are you?"

Noble glanced down at himself. "Do I look like a salesman?"

"No." The old guy stared past Noble. "Do I?"

"You from here?"

"Born and mostly raised."

"What brought you to New York?"

"Work."

"What kind of work was that?"

The older man turned and headed back to his truck. He looked over his shoulder. "Come on, follow me. Let's go grab a beer."

Noble returned to the Wrangler, shifted into first, and waited for the beaten-up truck to pull past him. He followed a few car lengths behind. The map of downtown formed in his mind, and he thought of every street that branched off of Main. Then he planned routes that branched off of those if he was led too far astray.

The truck's brake lights hardly shone through what must have been years of grit and grime built up on the plastic housings. The Wrangler screeched to a stop. The other man stuck his arm out and waved Noble up next to him.

"Go up four blocks and make a right. Place called Lacy's. Best bison burger you'll ever have. Grab two spots at the bar and I'll meet you there in fifteen."

Noble nodded. "Sounds good, friend."

The drive through eastern downtown had been uneventful. He took the four blocks well below the posted twenty-five miles per hour, studied each face he passed, hoped to see the only one he'd know in town. Most everyone he passed was older. It seemed like the minimum age to be a resident was somewhere in the sixties. There were a few groups of kids though. Young ones on bikes. Older ones on the corner. Had to be parents somewhere in town, too.

He glanced at his watch. Barely noon. What were the kids doing out? It wasn't a holiday. He passed a group of four that looked to be thirteen or fourteen, squished together on a bench outside a hardware store. They stared ahead, not interacting with one another. Arms and ankles crossed. It was only a few seconds, but Noble noted he was never that still at that age, especially when unsupervised.

The fourth cross street approached. Jack slowed, signaled, took in as much of the stretch of Main Street ahead as possible before turning right. Lacy's was a block away, on the left. He shifted out of gear and cruised the final hundred feet, cutting the wheel and coasting into an empty parking spot between two super duty trucks. Both white. Both with stickers along the body that read Leak Geeks Plumbing. Noble chuckled as he slid off his seat.

Gravel crunched underfoot as he made his way to the entrance. The front door was red, freshly-painted. A window was cut in the center of it, heavily-tinted, same as the windows to the side of the door. Was no one meant to see inside? For a moment, he wondered what kind of bar Lacy's might be. He shuttered the idea. Too close to the center of town for a strip club.

No one looked up at the stranger as Noble let the door fall shut. The bright slice of sunlight diminished into a tiny sliver that managed to sneak through the space between door and jamb. He strode to the bar. Took off his windbreaker. Set it on an empty stool and climbed onto the one next to it.

There were three empty stools to his right separating him from the only other patrons. The Leak Geeks themselves, he presumed. It took all of three seconds to determine they were father and son. The same heavy brow. The same Roman nose. The older one's hairline a few inches farther back than the younger's.

A woman in her mid-fifties came through the kitchen door and stopped in front of Noble. Lacy, he presumed. She asked, "Get you something?"

"Anything local on tap?"

She nodded and took a few steps toward the center of the bar and poured his beer. The tap handle read Highwoods American Wheat. He glanced at the chalkboard behind the bar and saw it was brewed by Big Spring Brewing right there in Lewistown.

He noted the lemon scent as he lifted the glass and took his first sip.

"Well?" the woman asked.

Noble nodded, wiped away the head on his upper lip. "I dig it. Hear you make a hell of a bison burger here."

She smiled. "That's what we're known for."

The older of the Leak Geek's straightened up. "Ah, hell, Lacy, you know you're known for your sweet smile and service."

"Fuck off, Ron," she said. It was met with laughter by the plumbers.

"Regulars?" Noble asked.

"Unfortunately," she said.

The room and Lacy's face lit up as the front door opened. She squinted against the sunlight. A smile formed as the light diminished. She nodded. "Benjamin. Good to see you."

Jack felt a strong hand land on his shoulder. He saw the older man in his peripheral as he swung his left leg over the stool and perched atop the seat.

"I see you've met my new friend," he said to the bar owner. He glanced at Jack's beer and nodded. "Good choice, but you really ought to try their scotch ale next." He redirected his focus to Lacy. "Pour me a Big Ern, would ya?"

She stepped to the side again.

"Benjamin," Jack said.

"Dunston. Ben Dunston. I never caught your name."

"Jack."

"Got a last name, Jack?"

"Jack's sufficient for now."

"Suppose it is." He took a sip of his scotch ale and gave Lacy a nod. "Fire me up one of them bison burgers?"

Jack stuck a finger in the air. "Put it all on my tab." He looked down the other end of the bar. "Their bill, too."

Lacy's smile faded into a disgusted look. "You really wanna cover those hooligans?"

Ben laughed. "Don't pretend like you didn't love that man just ten years ago."

Noble raised an eyebrow, but Lacy waved him off.

"Ancient history," she said. "Plus, he wasn't as fat back then."

The younger of the Leak Geeks got a laugh out of that one.

"Mom, don't rag on Dad so much. I gotta work with him the rest of the day."

"And you gotta live with him, too. Thank God it's not me stuck in the house with that man."

The elder Leak Geek smiled and shook his head. "Still in love with ya, woman."

She waved him off with a roll of her eyes and slipped back into the kitchen. The door swung back and forth a couple times before coming to rest. The bar quieted down for a few minutes as the men drained their mugs and ordered a second round.

Jack spoke up. "What's with all the kids on Main Street? It's not a holiday. Why aren't they in school?"

Ben's smile faded. He cleared his throat, took a moment before replying. "School's closed for the next week or so."

"They got termites or something?" Noble smiled, but the other man's face hardened.

Ben turned in his seat, draped his left arm over the bar, revealing a Panerai watch. "You really don't know?"

"Know what?"

"Shit, I figured that's why you were here. Thought they sent *you* to investigate the disappearance."

CHAPTER 2

A RIVER OF ICE SNAKED DOWN NOBLE'S BACK. ONE THOUGHT came to mind. One image. The same one he carried around everywhere he went.

Reese.

He resisted the urge to take out her picture and show it to Ben. If by chance it was Reese who had gone missing, he'd make himself a person of interest at the least by doing so. Possibly a suspect. The coincidence could not be ignored, though. He hesitated before replying, thinking through Ben's statement. The older man had assumed Noble was there to investigate. Who was this guy? Noble had done nothing to indicate his background, but Ben had picked up on the fact that Noble had a specific history.

What did that say about the older man?

Ben's eyes bore into Noble as he awaited a reply. This was a game Noble knew well. Ben wouldn't say a word until Noble spoke up.

"Investigate?" Noble forced a laugh. "Like I said, just passing through town. Planned on staying a couple days before continuing west to Bozeman."

Ben nodded, slapped Noble on the shoulder once and left his hand there. "Guess I read you wrong."

Noble couldn't let it lie there. He had to press for more information. Had to be subtle about it. "Was it a student?"

A sad smile formed on Ben's lips. "That went missing?"

"Yeah." Jack paused a beat. "Gotta be a pretty big deal in a small town like this."

"Wouldn't it be anywhere?"

"Connections are tighter in communities like this. Everyone knows someone who knows everyone. Tragedy hits harder, especially when it's a kid." Jack glanced over his shoulder and saw that the father and son at the other end of the bar had turned in his direction.

"That's true," Ben said. "Wasn't a kid, though. God, could you imagine?"

Jack could. It wasn't hard to retrieve the memory. He didn't delve into that part of his life, only nodded.

Ben continued. "A teacher by the name of Brenda Cresswell. Vanished. Name mean anything to you?"

Noble felt as though he were at the beginning of an interrogation. "Can't say I've ever heard of her."

"She went missing last week, after school, and I'm at my wits end trying to figure out where the hell she went. In my experience, people don't just vanish without a trace."

"You're a cop. I know you said you aren't, but it all adds up."

Ben shrugged. "Of sorts."

"That's what you did in New York?"

Ben offered a weak smile. "Sort of."

He wouldn't get any more out of the man. Not yet. Not until he offered something. "Tell me more about Brenda Cresswell."

"You the sort of guy who can help with this, Jack?"

It was Jack's turn to shrug. "You seem to think so. Let's leave it at that."

The older man sipped the head off his beer before taking a larger swig. He stared at Noble for several seconds, perhaps contemplating whether the stranger in front of him could be trusted, or if Jack might have information Ben could use. A small line of foam on his upper lip disappeared. There was something behind the guy's eyes. He wasn't a simple man, no matter what his truck or his clothing or even his worn holster looked like. Every line on his face held years of experience and wisdom.

"Can you give me a definitive answer, Jack?" Ben said. "Every minute matters. We're well past forty-eight hours now. I don't want to talk bad about anyone, but local law enforcement, well, they aren't exactly equipped for this."

The elder Leak Geek said, "They ain't equipped for nothing," and he and his son belly laughed at the joke.

"That's your brother and uncle you're talking about," Lacy said. "You'd do well to learn some respect for them."

The Leak Geeks waved her off.

Ben lifted a finger toward Lacy, and she waved him off.

"I'm only talking to those knuckleheads," she said. "You have a valid point. They aren't equipped for this and at least you know what that means."

"What's that mean?" Noble asked.

Ben tilted his head and glanced up at the ceiling. "State police or maybe even the FBI will come in and turn the town upside down. You probably know as well as I do that never leads to anything good."

Noble did. The FBI took Reese away from him years ago. It had taken several years for Noble to find her again, only to have her ripped away once more. Last thing he needed was the FBI showing up and realizing they were in the same town again. She'd be moved, and he'd have to start over.

"Place like this must have some secrets, huh?" Jack said.

"Too many," Lacy said. "And most people in Montana, well,

they don't like the government stepping onto their property, trouncing on their lives. Not the locals, the staties, or the feds. Always leads to upheaval. Upheaval leads to people pushing farther away from the middle. People pushing farther away from the middle leads to more tension. See, Jack, this place might look nice and quaint on the outside, but it's a tinder keg, and I'm telling you, it's close to exploding."

Noble drained his beer and slid the mug over to her, asked for another as he contemplated Lacy's words. How much of what she said had to do with Brenda Caldwell? Was this a woman she knew? Hell, how much of what she said had to do with herself? Was she stuck in the middle? Or was she being pulled farther away than she felt comfortable with.

Lacy set the beer down in front of him, leaned over the bar top. "Look, all I'm saying is, if Ben is right about you, think about sticking around and helping out. That woman needs it. Hell, this whole town needs it. You see what I'm saying?"

"Did you know her?" Jack asked. "Brenda Cresswell?"

Lacy shot a glance to the other end of the bar. It lasted less than a second, but it meant something. "Like you said, everyone here knows someone who knows everyone."

"Are you in the everyone group, or are you the someone?"

Lacy shrugged, stood upright, stepped back. She crossed her arms over her chest. "You help out Ben, maybe I'll tell you more."

The standoff lasted a couple of minutes before Lacy went back to the kitchen. The bar fell silent. Each man swiveled on his stool and stared straight ahead, thoughts dripping into the amber liquid in front of him.

"I'm only here for a few days," Noble said.

"What's your reason for coming to town?" Ben asked.

"I've got some bad news to deliver to someone who might live here."

"That'll take a few days?"

"Gotta find them first."

"I know most people here." Ben held his mug up to his lips. "Those I don't know, I can find. I could help you out."

"If I help you."

Ben nodded, tipped his glass up, and emptied the mug.

On cue, Lacy came through the door carrying two plates. She set them in front of Noble and Ben.

"Best bison burger in the state?" Jack said.

"In the damn country," Lacy said.

Jack took a bite, smiled, said through a mouth full of burger, "I think you're right. I mean, I've never had a bison burger before, but if I had, this would top any other in the country."

After they finished, Ben pushed his plate across the bar and turned to Jack. "Talk outside?"

"Sure." Jack dropped a fifty on the bar and followed the other man through the front door. The sun hovered over the building across the street, knifed through his eyes, distorted the view of his surroundings. He blinked a few times to adjust. "What do you have to say out here that you couldn't in there?"

"Don't trust those two at the end of the bar," Ben said.

"You catch that look Lacy exchanged with them when I asked if she knew Brenda Cresswell?"

Ben nodded. "Yup." He paused a beat. "Look, I'm not saying they're involved, but there's some connection there."

"That's the feeling I got." Noble leaned against his Wrangler. "How well do you know Lacy?"

"Well enough that I'd believe most of what she says."

"Did you believe her in there?"

"You're asking a lot of questions, Jack."

"Suppose I am."

"So what's it gonna be? You on board?"

"Suppose I am."

CHAPTER 3

CLOUDS ROLLED PAST OVERHEAD, THE SUN'S RAYS CATCHING an opening here and there. They thickened to the north. A storm was on its way.

Ben climbed into his truck and leaned out the open window. "I've got some errands to run. Head on over to the Lewiston Inn. Sam runs it. Tell him I sent you, and he'll take care of you. I'll drop by there this evening. We can grab some dinner and I'll fill you in on the case."

Jack nodded and waited until the man pulled out before climbing into the Wrangler. He pulled up his mental map and saw the layout of the town. The Lewiston Inn was three blocks west, one block south. The drive would take two minutes, max. Noble stretched it out to twenty, scoured the perimeter of town, the edge of the grid that contained seventy percent of the residents.

The houses were all similar. Craftsman style. Built in the earlier part of the 1900s. The lots were similar in size, but each presumably took on the characteristics of their owners. Some were meticulously kept. While others looked like nature had taken over. There were a lot of trucks and SUVs parked in driveways.

Noble saw fewer faces along the border of town. None were Reese. Those who spotted him waved and went on about their business. It was still early afternoon. Perhaps there would be more out and about later in the day.

He cut down a middle road toward Main Street and navigated to the Lewiston Inn. The building took up a quarter of a block and was situated on a corner. A sign fixed to the facade said there was parking in the rear. Noble drove around back and pulled into an empty spot in an empty row in an empty lot.

The hotel blocked the sunlight. A stiff breeze blew across the lot. It felt fifteen degrees cooler. Noble grabbed his bag from the back of the Wrangler and stood there for a moment, soaking in the atmosphere. Smoke rose from a building adjacent to the backside of the parking lot. A barbecue restaurant he couldn't recall the name of. The smell lingered in the air. He figured it would be a good place to eat later if Ben agreed.

As he headed toward the sidewalk, the rev of an engine caught his attention. He glanced to his left and saw a Chevy Blazer with a lightbar fixed to the roof speed up and come to a rolling stop about twenty feet away. Noble put his head down and turned right and kept walking toward the corner. The cop pulled up even and rolled down his window.

"New in town?" the cop said through the open window.

Jack kept walking, didn't look over.

"Talking to you, buddy." When Jack continued walking, the cop lurched forward ten feet or so, threw the Blazer in park and hopped out. He raced around the front of his vehicle and blocked Jack's path. His hand rested on his service pistol. "You got a problem with authority?"

Jack slowed up, stopped far enough away from the officer so the guy couldn't touch him. "No."

"Then why are you running from me?"

Jack laughed. "You call walking at a leisurely pace, running?"

"I don't need your smart ass—"

"Did I do something wrong? Jaywalk across the parking lot or something?"

"Well, no, but—"

"So you're harassing me just for shits and giggles then?" Jack noted the officer's name tag read Tilley.

"You got a mouth on you, you know that?" The cop's eyes narrowed, a storm of his own brewing in the furrowed lines of his forehead. "This is a quiet place and we like to keep it that way. Strangers stick out, especially those who don't stop when addressed by the law."

Jack met the officer's gaze. "Look, Tilley, I'm not trying to make waves. I'm here on personal business. Should be in and out in the matter of a few days."

"Personal business, huh?" He studied Jack for a few seconds, one eye squinted. "You got a name?"

"Jack."

"Jack what?"

"Sure."

"Huh?"

"Look, all you need to know is my name is Jack—" he hiked his thumb over his shoulder, "—that's my Jeep over there, and I'm gonna stay here at the Lewiston Inn for a couple days while I take care of my business. If you need to know more than that, find a reason to arrest me."

The officer's posture eased slightly, but his hand remained near his pistol. "All right, Jack. Best keep your guard up. Like I said, we don't like anyone disrupting our peaceful community." The cop's radio crackled to life, a voice calling for assistance on the other end. He glared at it, presumably torn between duty and the desire to assert his authority. "I'll be keeping an eye out. Don't cause any trouble."

Jack watched the deputy stride back to his Blazer. The

encounter left a sour taste in his mouth. He didn't need complications. Definitely not when he had a difficult task ahead. He turned the corner and made his way to the front of the Lewiston Inn, the brass of the door handle gleaming in a stray beam of sunlight that evaporated by the time his hand hit it.

Cool air billowed from a vent overhead. The lobby was a throwback to another era, with dark wood paneling and deep green carpeting. A hint of cigar smoke lingered. A grandfather clock ticked methodically in the corner. At the reception desk, a man in his late fifties with a head of thick silver hair looked up from his newspaper. "Help you?"

"You Sam? Ben Dunston sent me," Jack said. "I need a room."

The man nodded as he folded his newspaper and set it to the side. "You're in the right place, then." He stepped in front of his computer and tapped at the keyboard. "You want a room on a high floor?"

Jack stifled a smile. The place was only five stories high. He'd forgo the view of rooftops for the safety a lower floor offered. "First or second floor is fine with me."

"We have a nice suite on the second floor. Rumor is Franklin Roosevelt stayed there one summer back in the '20s." He turned around and opened up a wooden cabinet door, reached in and retrieved a key. Sam slid it across the counter. The tag attached read ROOSEVELT 214. "There's an elevator right over there." He gestured. "Or stairs if you go down that hallway right there. After five, I'll be manning the bar. Just walk past the elevators and find me. I make a mean Old Fashioned."

Jack couldn't help but feel the weight of the upcoming conversation with Reese as he pocketed the key. He'd need to be at his best, which meant rest. And sobriety. He thanked Sam and found the stairwell. The creak of the stairs beneath his boots served as a reminder that in towns like Lewistown, every step was noticed, every stranger a subject of curiosity or concern. He'd have to tread carefully.

Once inside his room, Jack set his bag down and moved to the window, peering out at the gathering clouds. He hoped the coming storm would be the only one he'd have to weather.

CHAPTER 4

JACK SHOOK OFF THE COBWEBS LEFT BEHIND FROM HIS NAP and spent a few seconds grounding himself in his new location. The room was simple, plain. A bed, chair, dresser, and nightstand. An alarm clock with large, bold numbers sat atop the nightstand. 5:30.

He went to the window, which looked over Main Street. The clouds had darkened and thickened while he slept, but the rain hadn't started yet. The sidewalks were livelier than earlier. People made their way in and out of the grocery store across the street. Tomorrow would bring more activity. Friday had a way of doing that. There was still tonight to deal with, so he put on his shirt and shoes and took the stairs to the lobby.

Sam greeted him at the bar, which was empty except for an older couple at the far end. There were a dozen pub tables spread throughout the room and booths lining the walls.

"Settling in?" Sam asked.

Jack nodded. "Ready for that Old Fashioned."

"Bourbon or Rye?"

"Rye." He pointed at the lineup of bottles set in front of an antique stained mirror. "Whistle Pig 12 year."

Sam nodded. "Good choice."

Jack watched as the man mixed the drink and poured it over a large ice cube. Sam slid it across the bar.

"What brings you to our little town?"

Jack hesitated before saying, "Looking for an old friend. Heard they were living here now."

Sam nodded, said nothing. His lips drew thin, and he avoided making eye contact.

Jack reached into his shirt pocket and pulled out a picture of Reese. He set it down in front of him. "She look familiar?"

Sam glanced down, shook his head. "Might be a small town, but that doesn't mean I know everybody. I keep my circle small, if you know what I mean." Before Jack could respond, Sam added, "Ben called about half an hour ago. Said he'll be here around six."

Jack hefted the drink to his lips, took a sip, said, "Good. That's enough time for you to make me another one of these."

He nursed his second drink, letting the smooth rye calm his nerves. It was five minutes to six. He had just enough time to savor the last sip when in walked Ben Dunston. The older man's presence was commanding, even in the casual attire of jeans and a flannel shirt. He waved to the older couple at the far end of the bar, then made his way over.

"Right on time." Jack stood to shake Ben's hand.

"Punctuality is a habit of mine." A slight smile tugged at the corners of his mouth. "Ready to dive into this?"

"All business," Jack said. "I like that. Saw a barbecue place behind the hotel. Figured we could talk over some ribs."

"Sounds like a plan."

They left the inn and walked the short distance to the restaurant, the air thick with the promise of rain.

The BBQ restaurant stood on its own. Its weathered brick facade a testament to the town's century-old history. The building, like many others in Lewistown, had seen countless seasons and stories pass through its doors. Its red bricks were faded and chipped in places.

Above the entrance, a vintage sign swung gently in the evening breeze. Its peeling paint still legible enough to read "Hank's BBQ" in bold, faded letters. The smell of smoked meat greeted them as they entered. The young woman at the stand took Jack in, smiled at Ben and told them to seat themselves. They found a booth in a corner that offered some privacy.

A few minutes later, a waitress named Shiela came over and greeted Ben by name. She set two bottles of beer down on the table, said, "Your usual, sir," and walked off.

"Friend of yours?" Jack asked.

"I may come in once or twice a month," Ben said.

There was laughter behind them. "Try once or twice a week," Sheila said. "He having what you're having, Ben?"

"Ribs?" Jack asked.

Ben nodded, said, "Yeah, double it up."

Jack leaned in. "All right, Ben. We can bullshit all night long, but I think it's better we just get down to it. What do you know about Brenda Cresswell's disappearance?"

Ben took a deep breath. "Brenda's a high school teacher. She's well-liked by her students and colleagues. She went missing last week. Last seen leaving the school around 5 pm. Her car was found abandoned on a back road about ten miles out of town, keys still in the ignition."

"You see the car?"

Ben nodded.

Jack took out a small notepad and jotted down some notes. "Any signs of a struggle?"

Ben shook his head. "None. The car was locked, and there was no blood or any obvious signs of foul play. It's like she just vanished into thin air."

"Her personal affects? In the car?"

"Her purse was in there, but it was empty. Brenda also carried a backpack. Maybe she dumped everything into that."

"What about her personal life? Any enemies? Someone with a motive?"

Ben sighed. "That's the thing. Brenda was well-loved. No known enemies. But she was involved in some community projects that might have ruffled a few feathers."

"Such as?"

"She was spearheading a campaign to protect some local land from being developed into a resort. The kind of place rich people could come out for a week and pretend they're roughing it, while all they're really doing is glamping. The developers weren't too happy about it."

"Was her car found near that land?"

Ben nodded. "Same road, few miles away."

Jack scribbled in his notebook. "Developers. Resort. Got it. Anyone specific?"

"Yeah, a guy named Carl Hennessey. He's been pushing hard for this project. Stands to make a lot of money if it goes through."

"Is Hennessey from here?"

"Sort of. His family..." Ben glanced over Jack's shoulder, straightened up.

Sheila set down two plates with baby back ribs hanging over the edges. She replaced their empty beers and then sauntered off.

Ben chuckled as he watched her go. "Almost got caught gossiping by the town gossip." He grabbed a bottle of barbecue sauce and applied it liberally to his ribs. "Seriously, it might be a good idea to talk to her later if we can get a lead or two."

"Why not now?"

"Already tried." Ben cut his ribs into manageable pieces. "She didn't have anything, and she's not particularly close to Brenda. Knows her because they were a couple years apart, but very little interaction since high school days."

Jack looked at the waitress and guessed her age to be late thirties. "Good twenty years then."

Ben nodded. "Anyway, back to Carl Hennessey."

"Right."

"His family has always been here, but he was shipped off to boarding school. Youngest of five children. An accident, if you will. Parents didn't want anything to do with him. They died. He came back for his inheritance and apparently spotted a gold mine of an opportunity here. Decided to build up the place."

"Has he succeeded?"

"A bit. This deal he's working on would pay him handsomely. Got a lot riding on it, I suppose."

"Definitely someone to talk to." Jack took a bite of his ribs and sat back, savoring the taste. He washed it down with a swig of beer.

"Let's tread carefully. But, yeah, he's on my radar."

"Anything else?" Jack asked between bites.

"Brenda had a close friend, a fellow teacher named Sarah. She's been pretty shaken up by all this. All she did was cry with me. I know her too well. Might be worth you talking to her, though. I'll give you her address."

Jack nodded. "I'll do that. What about the local cops? Are they doing anything?"

Ben's expression darkened. "They're trying, but they're out of their depth. And I get the feeling some of them might be in Hennessey's pocket."

"I had a run-in with one of them earlier. Tilley was his name."

Ben smirked. "I know him. Hell, he was at my house most every day back when he was a pimple-faced teenager. He give you a hard time?"

"He tried to bully me a bit. Left looking stupid."

Ben chuckled. "Sounds about right." His face turned somber. "Still, we should let them be. Once we have something, we can bring it to them. I figure the state police or even the FBI will get involved sooner than later. Something tells me the wind is about to carry this thing beyond the veiled walls of Lewiston."

Jack leaned back, processing everything. "All right, I'll start with Sarah. And I'll keep an eye on Hennessey. Anything else you can think of?"

Ben shook his head. "That's all I've got for now. But I'll keep digging."

They bantered about nothing much as they finished their dinner. Jack's mind was already plotting the next steps. The storm outside had finally broken, rain tapping against the windows like a thousand tiny fingers.

As they stood to leave, Ben reached into his pocket and retrieved his ringing phone. "Gotta take this." And as he walked toward the exit, Jack heard him say, "You gotta be kidding."

CHAPTER 5

JACK WOKE UP EARLY, THE FIRST RAYS OF DAWN FILTERING through the thin curtains of his room at the inn. The events of the previous day played on a loop in his mind, a constant reminder of the urgency of his mission. He stood and stretched. Felt the familiar weight of the investigation pressing down on him. Today he had to find Sarah and see if she could shed any light on Brenda's disappearance.

After a quick workout, he made his way downstairs. The inn's small dining area was just beginning to stir. Jack grabbed a quick breakfast of scrambled eggs, bacon, and a cup of black coffee. He ate mechanically as his thoughts raced ahead to the day's tasks. The food was good by hotel standards, but he barely tasted it. His mind was focused on piecing together the fragments of information he had gathered so far.

Every few minutes his thoughts would drift to Reese. He figured the more rapport he built with people in town would light the path to her door.

Jack finished his breakfast and reviewed his notes from the previous night. Sarah, Brenda's close friend, was his only lead. Ben had given him an address. Jack hoped Sarah could provide more details about Brenda's life and the people around her. Ben probably knew the information, but for whatever reason, the older man wanted Jack to hear it firsthand. Figure things out on his own.

The morning air was crisp as Jack drove through the quiet streets of the town. It was still early. Only a few people were out and about. He made his way to the outskirts of town beyond the main grid where Sarah lived. The houses here were modest, with well-tended yards and gardens.

Jack arrived at a small ranch with a neatly trimmed lawn and a few potted plants by the front door. He took a moment to observe the surroundings. The neighborhood was peaceful and there was nothing out of the ordinary. He approached the door and knocked, the sound echoing in the stillness of the morning, eliciting a bark from a nearby dog.

After a few moments, the door opened, and a woman in her mid-to-late-thirties stood before him. Her eyes were red-rimmed with dark circles beneath. Tear paths stained her cheeks like dried creek beds.

"Sarah?"

She clutched the edges of her robe as she looked past him, down the street in both directions. Her gaze finally settled on him. "Yes? Do I know you?"

"No, you don't. Ben sent me. Name's Jack. I'm looking into what happened to Brenda. Ben thought you might be able to help."

Sarah's expression softened at the mention of Brenda's name. At the same time, a fresh layer of tears covered her eyes. "You're a friend of Ben's?"

Jack nodded.

She hesitated for a moment, then stepped aside to let Jack in. "Come in."

Jack followed her into the living room, a cozy space filled with photos of family and dogs and other mementos. As they sat down,

Jack could see the strain on Sarah's face. This wouldn't be easy for her, but he needed help to piece together the puzzle of Brenda's disappearance.

"I know this is difficult, but anything you can tell me about Brenda and what was happening in her life could be crucial to locating her."

Sarah nodded, taking a deep breath. "I'll do my best," she said, her voice wavering. "Brenda was my best friend. I want to help find her. It's not like her to disappear. She'd text me when she was going grocery shopping so someone knew where she was."

Jack leaned forward, his attention focused entirely on Sarah. "Did she text you the day she disappeared?"

"I mean, yeah, but not to, like, tell me she was heading ten miles outside of town."

"OK. Let's start with the basics. When was the last time you saw Brenda?"

Sarah took a deep breath. She winced, and a tear slipped over her eyelid and snaked down her cheek. She pushed past the pain of the memories. "It was the day before she disappeared. We met for coffee at the usual place, just to catch up. She seemed ... off. More stressed than usual."

"Stressed about what?" Jack asked.

"This project."

"The resort? Land development?"

Sarah nodded, said, "Brenda was really passionate about it. She wanted to protect the local wildlife and the community. So much has changed here in the past two decades. She was always talking about how it would ruin the town, and she was organizing protests, writing letters, you name it. She was dedicated, almost to the point of obsession."

"Anything else unusual about her behavior?"

Sarah hesitated. "She was also worried about her students. She taught at the local high school, you know. And I'm telling you, she cared about those kids like they were her own. She mentioned that some of them were having a tough time, and she was trying to help them as much as she could. It was like she was carrying the weight of the world on her shoulders."

"Did she ever mention any student in particular?"

Sarah glanced away. "She was always careful not to reveal too much personal information about her students. The situations were always generalized, and aside from saying he or she, she gave no other identifying information."

"Could any of those situations put her in harm's way?"

"I guess it's possible, but I really wouldn't know."

Jack's mind raced as he processed this information. Brenda's dedication to her causes and students could have made her some enemies, but he needed more specifics. "Was there anyone in particular who might have had a reason to harm her?"

Sarah's face grew even more somber. "There was one person. Her ex-boyfriend, Mark Cundiff. He was ... possessive. Obsessive, even. They broke up over a year ago, but he never really let it go. At first, it was typical post-breakup stuff. We figured he'd move on soon enough. But then he started showing up places where she'd be, leaving notes on her car, her front door, even her desk at school. He was calling her at all hours. It got to the point where Brenda was genuinely scared of him."

"What else can you tell me about Mark?"

Sarah paused for a moment. "He's in his late thirties, tall, with short brown hair and a bit of a scruffy beard. He used to work in construction, but I'm not sure what he's doing now. Brenda tried to get a restraining order, but it didn't make much difference. He'd still find ways to get close to her."

"Where can I find him?"

Sarah shrugged. "He moved shortly after they split up and I'm not sure where he lives now. I've seen him around town a few times." Her voice trembled. "He hangs out at a few different bars, and sometimes he's at the gym. He's not exactly hiding, but he's not easy to pin down either."

"Anything else you can tell me about him? Any incidents that stand out?"

Sarah's eyes filled with tears again. "There was one night, a few weeks ago. Brenda found a note on her car, a really creepy one. It said something like, 'You can't hide from me.' She showed it to me, and we both knew it was from Mark. She was terrified, but she didn't want to go to the police again. She thought it would just make things worse."

Jack felt a chill run down his spine. This was the kind of lead he needed, but it also painted a grim picture of Brenda's last days. "Thanks, Sarah. This helps a lot. I'm gonna track Mark down."

Sarah nodded, wiping her eyes. "Please, find her. She doesn't deserve this."

Jack stood and offered her a reassuring smile. "I'll do everything I can." He exited the house and got in his Jeep. But before turning it on, Sarah ran out the door toward him.

"I almost forgot," she said.

"What is it?"

"The day Brenda disappeared, I was out for a run. I went by the school, and I swear I saw Mark drive by in a blue Ford F-150."

"Blue F-150," Jack said. "Got it."

As he pulled away from the house, he couldn't shake the feeling that someone was watching him.

CHAPTER 6

JACK NEEDED MORE INFORMATION FOLLOWING HIS VISIT WITH Sarah. He needed to talk to someone who had their fingers on the pulse of the town. One name came to mind.

Lacy.

He meandered through town, past his hotel. A few turns later and he'd arrived. He parked his Jeep outside Lacy's bar, taking a moment to gather his thoughts before heading inside. It'd be best to ease into the questions. Ask too much too quickly, and she'd shut him down.

He pulled the door open and took in the scene. The bar was slow, with a few locals perched on stools at the counter and a couple seated at a table, engaged in quiet conversation. The familiar neon sign buzzed softly, casting a warm glow over the entrance. He took a deep breath. The weight of the investigation pressed down on him. He was determined to uncover more leads.

The door fell shut behind him. He was greeted by the comforting scent of grilled food and the low hum of casual chatter. The dim lighting and rustic decor gave the place a cozy, welcoming atmosphere. Jack scanned the room, noting the regulars who blended seamlessly into the background of the bar's well-worn interior.

Jack approached the bar and caught Lacy's eye. She greeted him with a raised eyebrow, clearly remembering him from his previous visit. Her eyes sparkled with a mix of recognition and intrigue as she wiped down the counter with a practiced hand.

"Well, look who's back," she said with a wink. "What can I get you this time?"

Jack slid onto a stool and leaned forward slightly. "I'll take a beer, the scotch ale this time. And another bison burger, medium, the works."

"Ah, you enjoyed that, did you?"

"That was one of the best meals I've had in a while. And, not for nothing, I drove up here from Austin, Texas."

Lacy chuckled, nodding as she turned to grab a pint glass. "I'll take that as a compliment. Have you tried Hank's yet? If you're staying at the Lewiston Inn, it's adjacent to the parking lot."

Jack took note that she mentioned the hotel, but he knew there weren't many in town. "Ate there last night with Ben. Pretty damn good."

As she poured his drink, Jack eased into the conversation with some small talk. "How are things around here on a Friday night? Seems pretty quiet now."

Lacy placed the frothy beer in front of him and leaned on the counter, her smile widening. "Oh, Fridays are a whole different story. Lots of fun, good crowd, live music sometimes. You should come by tonight if you're looking for a good time."

Jack took a sip of his beer, savoring the cold, crisp taste. "Sounds like a plan. I might just do that."

Lacy nodded approvingly as she moved to check on another customer. Jack took the opportunity to glance around the bar again, his mind raced with the questions he needed to ask. He had to tread carefully. Gaining Lacy's trust and getting the information he needed without raising too many suspicions was crucial.

When Lacy returned with his burger, Jack decided it was time to steer the conversation toward the reason for his visit. "I was hoping you could help me out with something, Lacy."

Lacy raised an eyebrow. "What's that?"

Jack took another sip of his beer, choosing his words carefully. "I'm looking into a couple of people—Mark Cundiff and Carl Hennessey. Heard they might come around here sometimes."

Lacy's expression shifted as she narrowed her eyes. "Mark Cundiff? Yeah, I know him. He's a regular here, but not exactly the kind of guy you'd want to be friends with."

Jack leaned in, sensing he was on the right track. "What do you mean?"

Lacy set her cleaning rag aside. "Mark's got a bit of a reputation. He's a troublemaker, always looking for a fight, especially after he's had a few drinks. And he's got this obsessive streak, particularly when it comes to his Brenda."

"Obsessive how?"

Lacy sighed, glancing around to make sure no one was eavesdropping. "This is far deeper than I want to get into with you."

"I'm working with Ben, trying to figure this thing out. Any information you have could help."

"Why not let the police handle it?"

"You said yourself yesterday they aren't any help."

Lacy nodded. "Mark used to follow her around, show up uninvited, that sort of thing. Brenda had to get a restraining order against him, but it didn't seem to stop him much. He's been in here more than once, ranting about how she did him wrong."

"And he's been in recently?"

"Yeah." Lacy lowered her voice. "Last time I saw him, he looked more agitated than usual. Kept muttering to himself, drinking like he was trying to forget something."

"When was that?"

"Earlier this week."

"He show up here often?"

"Probably be here tonight, if we're unlucky."

Jack filed that away for later. "What about Carl Hennessey?"

Lacy's brow furrowed in thought. "Carl's a different story. He's quiet, keeps to himself. Comes in late at night, usually sits in the corner nursing a drink while playing around on his laptop. Doesn't cause trouble, but you can tell he's got his own demons."

"What kind of background does he have?" Jack asked.

"Used to work in construction, from what I hear," Lacy replied. "But he's got a bit of a shady past. Rumors about some run-ins with the law, but nothing I can confirm. I've seen him and Mark talking a few times in here, but I wouldn't say they're friends. More like two guys who share a common misery."

Jack nodded. "Thanks, Lacy. This helps a lot."

Lacy gave him a curious look. "You're not just here for a burger and a beer, are you?"

Jack appreciated her perceptiveness. "No, I'm not. But I appreciate the hospitality."

Lacy shrugged, a hint of a smile playing on her lips. "Just be careful, Jack. This town has its secrets, and not all of them are worth uncovering."

Jack nodded, finished his beer and gestured for a refill. "I'll keep that in mind."

She grabbed a fresh glass and filled it. "Will you?"

"What?"

"Keep that in mind?" She placed her hands on the bar top and leaned in. "Brenda's not the first person to go missing here. It's not what you'd call a common occurrence, but it happens sometimes. So I'm just saying, if you find yourself getting in too deep, don't hesitate to call for help. The police are here for a reason."

"Thanks for your concern. If I feel threatened, I'll back off."

Lacy looked him in the eye. "You know, someone mentioned you were asking around about a woman. What's that about?"

Jack realized Sam must have mentioned something but didn't confirm it directly. "Yeah, I've been trying to track someone down. Who told you about that?"

Lacy gave a small shrug. "Small town, word gets around. So, who is this woman?"

Jack reached into his pocket and pulled out the picture of Reese, sliding it across the counter to Lacy. "Someone from my past that I need to give some news to. Do you recognize her?"

Lacy picked up the photo and studied it for a moment before her eyes widened in recognition. "That's Tanya. She comes in here often, usually on Friday nights. She keeps to herself mostly, but she's friendly enough. Likes to sit in the corner, away from the crowd. She's been coming here for a while now. If you're looking to talk to her, tonight's your best bet."

"She comes in alone?"

Lacy's smile returned. "If you are asking whether she has a man friend, I believe the answer is no."

Jack nodded, feeling a mix of relief and anticipation. "Thanks, Lacy. I'll be back tonight."

As he stood to leave, the door to the bar swung open with a loud creak, drawing everyone's attention. A man in his late-thirties stumbled in, disheveled and out of breath. His eyes darted around the room until they landed on Jack.

"Are you Jack?" the man asked. His voice trembled.

He'd been here a day and already people were looking for him. "Yeah, that's me. Who the hell are you?"

The man took a shaky step forward, clutching a crumpled piece of paper in his hand. "Tom. Heard you were looking into Brenda's disappearance. I've got something you need to see."

Jack met the man in the middle of the room and took the paper from Tom's hand. He unfolded it, revealing a hastily scrawled note that sent chills down his spine.

"Meet me at the old sawmill tonight. Come alone. — B"

Jack's mind raced. Brenda? Was she still alive? He looked up at Tom, who seemed genuinely terrified.

"Where did you get this?" Jack said.

Tom swallowed hard. "It was slipped under my door this morning. I don't know who left it, but after talking to Sarah, I thought you should have it."

Jack's pulse quickened. He glanced back at Lacy.

"The old sawmill is on the outskirts of town," she said. "Been abandoned for years. Nothing around it for a mile in any direction."

It was the perfect location for a trap. And it was Jack's only lead. He turned back to further interrogate Tom, but the man had given him the slip. The door fell shut.

Lacy leaned in, her expression serious. "Jack, this could be dangerous. You need to be careful."

"Who was that guy? You know him?"

"I know everybody."

"And?"

"You should ask Ben."

"I'll do that."

He turned to leave. As he stepped out into the warm afternoon air, he couldn't shake the feeling that he was walking into something far more sinister than he'd anticipated.

CHAPTER 7

JACK STOOD IN THE DIMLY LIT LOBBY OF THE LEWISTON INN, his mind racing as he replayed the events of the past few hours. The note from Tom, hastily scribbled and cryptic, weighed heavily in his pocket. He had to make a decision, and he needed Ben's input to ensure he wasn't making a grave mistake. As he saw Ben's familiar silhouette enter the lobby, he took a deep breath and steeled himself for the conversation ahead.

Jack waved Ben over and they entered the empty bar area, away from prying eyes and ears. Ben's expression was a mix of curiosity and concern. His eyes scanned Jack's face for clues.

"What's this all about, Jack?" Ben's voice was voice low and steady.

Jack reached into his pocket and pulled out the crumpled note. Handed it to Ben. "Tom slipped this to me at Lacy's bar. Says Brenda might be at the old sawmill tonight. Wants me to come alone. Lacy told me to ask you about Tom."

Ben unfolded the note, his brow furrowing as he read the scrawled message. "Tom, huh? Did he say anything else?"

"Not much," Jack said. "He looked terrified, like he was being watched. Said the note was slipped under his door this morning. He bolted before I could ask more."

"Tom's a good guy." Ben folded the note and handed it back. "Works down at the hardware store. He's reliable but scares easy. If he says this was slipped under his door, then it probably was. But that doesn't mean we should take this at face value."

"Signed like that, could it be Brenda? You think there's a chance she's in hiding?"

Ben paced to the end of the bar and back. "She doesn't strike me as the type to go it alone. If she needed help, I think she would have said something sooner."

Jack nodded. "If there's even a chance Brenda's there—"

"We can't ignore it," Ben finished Jack's thought. "But we can't rush in blind either. The sawmill's a perfect place for an ambush. Remote, abandoned. If someone wanted to set a trap, that's where they'd do it."

Jack sighed, ran a hand through his hair. "I know. But we don't have much time. We need to decide our next move."

They moved to a nearby table, sat down to weigh their options. The inn's quiet ambiance seemed to amplify the gravity of their discussion.

Jack spoke first. "We have two choices. We either go to the bar to gather more information and see if Mark or Carl are there. We can't be in two places at once."

Ben leaned back. "If we go to the bar, we might gather more intel on Mark and Carl. But if the note's legit and we miss the chance to find Brenda—"

Jack nodded. "Exactly. If Brenda's there and we don't show up, we might never get another lead like this."

"We could split up," Ben said. "One of us goes to the sawmill, the other to the bar."

Jack shook his head. "No way. It's too dangerous. If it is a trap, we need to be together. Strength in numbers."

Ben sighed. "You're right. The sawmill it is. We'll go together, but we need to be prepared for anything. But first, let's pay a visit to Tom."

"Let's gear up and head out. We don't have much time before nightfall."

Ben nodded, his expression resolute. "I'll meet you at your Jeep in ten."

As Jack and Ben walked out to the parking lot, they spotted Tom hanging around Jack's Jeep, nervously glancing around. His jittery demeanor did little to inspire confidence, but Jack knew they needed every piece of information they could get.

"Tom," Jack called out. "You got more to tell us?"

Tom jumped at Jack's voice, then nodded rapidly. "Yes, yes. I swear the note is genuine. Earlier, I took a drive. I saw some people around the sawmill. They were moving equipment, like they were setting something up."

Ben stepped forward. "What kind of people? Did you recognize any of them?"

Tom shook his head. "No, they were strangers to me. But they looked ... professional, you know? Not the kind of folks who just wander into town."

Jack exchanged a glance with Ben. "What else did you see, Tom? Any vehicles, anything that stood out?"

Tom rubbed his hands together, glancing around as if expecting someone to leap out of the shadows. "There was a black SUV, tinted windows. Couldn't see the plates. They were unloading stuff, big crates and tools. I didn't stick around to see more. Just got out of there and came to find you."

Jack placed his hand on Tom's shoulder and squeezed. "You did the right thing, Tom. We'll get to the bottom of this."

Tom nodded, sighed. "Be careful out there. Something about this feels off."

"We will," Ben said. "You get home and lock your doors. We'll take it from here."

The drive to the sawmill was tense. The setting sun cast long, eerie shadows across the landscape. Jack kept his eyes on the road, his mind racing with possibilities. Beside him, Ben methodically checked their gear, ensuring they were prepared for whatever awaited them.

"This feels like a setup," Ben said, breaking the silence. "Everything about it screams trap. You start poking around, and then there's a note."

Jack nodded. "I know. But we can't afford to ignore it. If there's even a chance Brenda's there, we gotta check it out."

Ben grunted in agreement. "What's your take on this? You think Brenda's hiding out or being held there?"

"I don't know," Jack admitted. "But either way, someone wants us to think she's there. We need to be ready for anything. Including the possibility that she's not there at all."

As they neared the sawmill, Jack's thoughts drifted to Reese. The danger she could be in if this situation reached her was a constant weight on his mind. He couldn't shake the feeling that everything was connected, that finding Brenda might be the key to finding Reese.

They arrived at the sawmill as dusk settled in, casting the dilapidated structure in a haunting light. The building was a relic. Its wooden beams creaked in the wind. Broken windows like empty eyes stared out into the darkness.

Jack parked the Jeep a safe distance away and they approached on foot. The crunch of gravel under their boots was the only sound. The stillness of the night amplified their tension. Jack tightened his grip on his flashlight, his other hand resting on the handle of his concealed weapon.

Ben gestured toward the entrance, a grim look on his face. "Stay sharp. We don't know what we're walking into."

They moved silently, each step bringing them closer to the ominous building. The sawmill was surrounded by overgrown vegetation, its walls marked with years of neglect. As they reached the door, a sudden noise from within made them freeze. It was faint, almost imperceptible, but enough to put them on high alert.

Jack and Ben moved cautiously around the perimeter of the sawmill, their flashlights cutting through the darkness. The wind whispered through broken windows. Every step was deliberate, every sound amplified in the stillness of the night.

Jack's flashlight beam swept across the ground. There were footprints in the dirt. He knelt down, examining them closely. "These are recent. We're not alone."

Ben nodded. "Over here."

Jack moved to Ben's side. A still-burning cigarette butt was on the ground. The acrid smell of tobacco lingered in the air mixed with the scent of old wood and decay. Ben crouched down, scanned the area. "They might've seen us walk up."

They continued their cautious sweep, peering through the broken windows and listening for any signs of movement. The faint noises from inside the sawmill grew more distinct—whispers, the creak of floorboards. Jack had the unmistakable feeling of being watched.

He exchanged a look with Ben. "We're *definitely* not alone."

Ben's jaw tightened. "Stay close. We need to be ready for anything."

As they prepared to enter the sawmill, loud noise shattered the silence. Jack and Ben froze, their flashlights fixed on the entrance. The door to the sawmill swung open with a groan, revealing a figure silhouetted against the dim light inside.

Jack drew his pistol.

The figure stepped forward.

Jack's breath caught in his throat. It was a face he hadn't expected to see out here, a face that brought a flood of memories rushing back. The figure moved into the light, revealing features twisted in a mix of fear and determination.

Jack and Ben stood rooted to the spot. They stared in shock and suspense. The moment stretched out, heavy with anticipation and unanswered questions.

"Jack?"

Jack's mind raced, struggling to process what he was seeing. "Reese?"

CHAPTER 8

JACK STOOD FROZEN, HIS FLASHLIGHT TREMBLING IN HIS hand as he stared at the figure before him. Reese stood in the dim light, her eyes wide with a mix of fear and relief. Beside him, Ben's grip tightened on his weapon, his body tense and ready for anything.

"Tanya?" Ben said. "The hell are you doing out here?"

She ignored him, her stare fixed on Jack.

"Reese?" Jack's voice was barely a whisper. He knew he'd find her. It was all he thought about since leaving Austin. But seeing her in front of him, the woman he at one time thought he'd never see again, left him in shock as disbelief and hope warred within him.

"Jack." Her voice trembled. "I can't believe it's really you."

Emotions surged through Jack as he stepped closer. He glanced around. Searched for any sign something was amiss. "What are you doing here?"

"I got a tip," Reese said. "It said there might be something here connected to Brenda's disappearance. I had to check it out."

Ben remained wary, his eyes never leaving Reese. "Who gave you the tip? Why didn't you tell anyone?"

Reese shook her head. "It came anonymously. I didn't know who to trust, and I didn't want to put anyone else in danger. I thought I could handle it. I mean, Jack, you know my background..."

"What's your connection with Brenda?"

"She's been my best friend here."

Jack glanced at Ben, who nodded. "Why didn't you mention her? Why Sarah instead?"

Ben shrugged. "We woulda got to her, I suppose."

Jack closed the distance between him and Reese. He reached out and took her hand. "We need to find out what's going on here."

Ben's jaw tightened, but he nodded. "Fine. But we stay sharp. This could still be a setup."

"I'm certain it is." He looked Reese in the eye. "Why would Tom have received a note to show up here, too?"

Reese shook her head. "Tom works for Carl Hennessey."

"We should sweep the place and get out," Ben said.

They moved cautiously into the sawmill. Their flashlights cast long shadows on the walls. The interior was even more dilapidated than it appeared from the outside. The smell of decay and neglect hung heavy in the air, mingled with the faint scent of recent human activity.

Jack's flashlight swept across the ground and revealed discarded food wrappers and a makeshift sleeping area. "Looks like someone's been staying here."

Reese knelt beside a pile of blankets. Her fingers brushed against a familiar scarf. "This is Brenda's." Her voice was tight with emotion. "She was here."

Ben's flashlight beam found a map of the town pinned to the wall, marked with several red X's. He studied the map. "Looks like someone's been planning something."

Jack joined him, his eyes narrowed as he examined the marks

and matched them up with his mental map. "These are key locations in town. What's the connection?"

Before anyone could answer, a faint noise reached their ears—a whisper of movement, the creak of a floorboard. Jack's heart pounded as he signaled for silence, his senses strained to catch any hint of danger.

"Easy goes it," Ben whispered.

They moved deeper into the sawmill, every step cautious and deliberate. The building closed in around them, the darkness growing thicker, more oppressive. Jack's flashlight caught a glimpse of something on the floor—a still-burning cigarette butt.

"Someone's close."

The trio pressed on. As they rounded a corner, the sound of hushed voices reached them. They grew louder with each step. Jack exchanged a tense look with Ben and Reese.

The sawmill was a maze of shadows and hidden threats, but they couldn't turn back now. Brenda's life—and perhaps their own—depended on what they found here.

Jack led the way, flashlight in one hand, his other ready on his weapon. Every sense was on high alert. The sawmill was a labyrinth of dark corridors and abandoned machinery, each corner holding the potential for danger.

"What's that?" Ben said.

Jack followed the man's outstretched arms and saw a couple of old wooden crates. "Just some crates."

"No, look closer. There's a seam in the floor."

Jack kicked the crates aside and discovered a hidden door. He pushed it open, revealing a staircase down to a basement. He motioned for Ben and Reese to follow. Their footsteps echoed on the creaky steps like tiny hammer falls.

The basement was a stark contrast to the decayed upper floors. It was filled with modern equipment and neatly organized documents. Blueprints and maps covered one wall, detailing the land development plans Jack presumed Brenda had been fighting against. He scanned the room. The evidence indicated this was a well-funded operation.

"This is it," Reese whispered, her eyes wide. "This is what Brenda was up against."

A noise behind them made Jack spin around. Two armed men stood at the entrance to the basement, guns drawn.

"Hands up!" one of them barked.

A tense standoff ensued. Jack and Ben raised their hands slowly, their eyes locked on the intruders. Reese remained still.

"We don't want any trouble," Jack said. "We're just here looking for answers."

The second man stepped closer. "Ain't never met a trespasser not looking for trouble."

Ben lunged at the nearest guard. The old man moved faster than Jack would've guessed. It surprised the guard, too. Ben knocked the gun from his hand. Jack followed suit, disarming the second guard with a swift move. Reese grabbed one of the fallen guns, trained it on the guards.

"Who sent you?" Jack said.

One of the guards, now bleeding from a gash on his forehead, spat at him. "You'll never make it out of here alive."

Jack pressed harder. "Who sent you? Why was Brenda taken? Where is she?"

When the guy didn't answer, Jack kicked him in the stomach, then turned to the other guy.

The guard hesitated, then muttered, "Carl Hennessey. She knew too much. She had evidence that could ruin him and his partners. Local officials, businessmen—they're all in on it."

Reese's grip tightened on the gun. "Where is Brenda now?"

The guard shook his head. "I don't know. But if you don't get out of here, you'll be joining her soon."

Jack and Ben exchanged a grim look. They had the information they needed, but now they had to get out alive. Jack gathered as many documents as he could carry, shoving them into his bag.

"We need to move, now," Jack said.

"What about them?" Ben said.

"Not a fan of leaving them alive," Jack said.

"Please," the bleeding guard said. "You'll get no trouble from us."

"Wallets." Jack aimed his pistol at the guy. "Both of you, throw your wallets to her."

They did as instructed. Reese scooped the wallets up and rifled through them. She tossed the cash and credit cards on the ground, held up their driver's licenses.

"Now we know exactly who you are and where you live," Jack said. "Won't take us long to find every living member of your family. So think twice about saying anything about tonight."

They turned to leave, only to hear more footsteps from above.

"We've got company," Ben said.

The bleeding guard pointed to the far wall. "There's a second way out. Takes you to ground."

Jack scanned the room. His eyes landed on an old piece of machinery. "We can use this to create a diversion."

They hurried to set up their makeshift trap, positioning the machinery to block the entrance to the basement. As the footsteps grew louder, Jack pulled the lever and sent the heavy equipment crashing down. The blocked doorway bought them precious seconds.

"Go, go!" Jack urged as he led the way out.

The sawmill erupted into chaos. The newcomers banged on the blocked door and shouted for them to open up.

Jack burst out into the night, the cool air hitting his face like a splash of water. Behind them, the sawmill was a cacophony of noise and confusion.

"This way!" Ben pointed toward the dense woods nearby.

The trio ran. The night air filled with the sounds of their ragged gasps. The commotion from their pursuers faded as they disappeared into the trees. The darkness swallowing them up.

For now, they were safe. But the conspiracy they had unearthed was far from over.

CHAPTER 9

THE SMELL OF BEER AND BURGERS SENT JACK'S STOMACH into a tailspin as he entered Lacy's bar with Ben and Reese behind him. He looked around the dimly lit room for any sign of Carl Hennessey or Mark Cundiff. The low hum of conversation filled the room. The Leak Geeks and a few other regulars sat at the bar and scattered tables, but there was no sign of their targets.

"See anything?" Ben asked, his voice low.

Jack shook his head. "No, but let's not hang around at the door too long. We don't want to draw attention."

Reese nodded. "Let's find a quiet spot where we can talk." She pointed at an empty table against the wall. "Over there."

They made their way to a table off to the side, partially hidden from the main area by a wooden partition. It offered a clear view of the entrance. They settled in, each taking a moment to scan the room one last time.

"Looks like we're in the clear for now." Jack signaled a waitress he hadn't seen before.

As they waited, the tension at the table eased. The waitress arrived. They ordered three beers and three bison burgers.

"We need to go over everything we found at the sawmill," Ben said once the waitress had left. "Piece together the connections and figure out our next move."

Jack pulled out the documents they had gathered, spreading them across the table. Reese leaned in. Her eyes flitted back and forth as she scanned the blueprints and maps while Ben kept an eye on their surroundings.

"These blueprints show significant land development plans." Jack pointed to the various red Xs marked on the map.

"It matches the locations Brenda was concerned about," Reese said. "She mentioned some of these to me. She believed Hennessey and his partners were planning something big, something illegal."

"Like this was a front?" Jack asked.

"Of sorts," Reese said. "She said they were laundering money, but it didn't stop there. At least one of these developments would house something illegal. Sorry, I can't give more detail than that. She wouldn't elaborate when I pushed."

"So was it a feeling? Or do you think she had more evidence?" Jack asked.

"She was abducted over it," Reese said. "I'm guessing she had more than a feeling."

Ben traced a finger along the lines connecting the various locations. "Look at this. It's a network. These spots aren't random. They're strategically placed."

Jack leaned back, his mind racing. "Brenda must have found evidence of their plans and was trying to stop them. That's why they took her."

Reese's eyes filled with tears. "We need to find her before it's too late."

Ben glanced around the bar again. "We should keep our voices down. This place has ears."

They continued to review the documents for a few more minutes, piecing together the conspiracy. The maps and blueprints revealed a coordinated effort to take over significant portions of land. A few of the documents indicated they were using underhanded methods and corrupt officials to push through their plans.

But for what? And why? That's what Jack needed to know.

The waitress returned with their drinks and food. The distraction was welcome. They took a moment to eat and drink, but their minds were still focused on the task at hand.

Reese broke the silence. "What's our next move?"

"We need more evidence," Jack said. "Something concrete that we can take to the authorities. This is good, but we need to know what they're doing that's illegal. And we need to find out where Brenda is being held."

Ben nodded. "We need to be careful. If Carl Hennessey gets wind of what we're doing, he'll come after us with everything he's got."

"I'm not afraid of Hennessey," Jack said.

"You might want to exercise some caution, Jack," Ben said. "I got a feel for who you are, but you don't know everything about this guy."

"Maybe we can find someone here who knows something," Reese suggested. "Lacy might have heard something."

Jack nodded. "It's worth a shot. Let's finish up here and then talk to her."

Ben wiped his hands on his napkin and retrieved his cell phone. He stood up and dropped a fifty on the table. "I'm going to follow up on this message I just got. There's a guy I know who might have more information on Hennessey's operations. I'll regroup with you later."

Jack nodded. "Stay safe. We'll keep digging here."

Ben leaned in. "Watch your backs. And keep your voices down. Like I said, this place has ears." With that, he slipped out of the bar, leaving Jack and Reese alone at the table.

Reese watched him go, then turned to Jack, her eyes searching his. She bit her bottom lip, took another sip of her beer. "It's been a long time, Jack."

The weight of their shared past hung heavy between them.

"It has," he said. "Too long."

"When you found me in Texas, I thought that was it. You and me, together. It was all I wanted since just after we first met. Can you believe how long ago that was?"

"Over a decade. Texas was, what, four years now?" He looked over her shoulder and signaled for the waitress. "Did they send you here right after?"

"No. Omaha for two years."

"Nebraska?"

"You got it."

"Terrible."

Reese laughed. Her smile lingered. "Can't believe you're here."

"Wish it was under better circumstances."

The tension between them eased as they talked. Jack found himself opening up to her, recounting the events that had happened after he was taken from her in Texas. "After they grabbed me, I was moved around a lot," he began. "Ended up in Europe for a while. Some old case that had resurfaced. Then I assumed the identity of a hitman to survive. Had two organizations after me. Total mess."

"That sounds dangerous."

"You seem shocked." He laughed, but the moment faded quickly. "I was constantly looking over my shoulder, wondering if today was the day they'd finally catch up to me."

Reese leaned forward, her gaze intense. "What kind of missions did they have you on?"

Jack sighed, running a hand through his hair. "All kinds. Assassinations, intel gathering, sabotage. They didn't care how dangerous it was, as long as it served their interests."

"And you just did it?" Reese asked, her voice filled with disbelief.

"I didn't have much of a choice," Jack said. "It was either that or get killed myself. I had to play along until I could find a way out. And I mean, a way out of it all."

Reese reached across the table, taking his hand in hers. "I'm so sorry, Jack. I had no idea what you were going through."

"It's in the past now." Jack squeezed her hand. "There's something I need to tell you."

"You're pregnant." She smiled wide, but Jack didn't return the gesture. Reese pulled away from his grasp and leaned back in her chair. "What is it?"

"Your brother."

Reese glanced around. "I spoke with him a few months ago. I know I shouldn't but—"

"Reese, I don't know how to say this, so I'm just going to do it. He died. In L.A., helping me."

"What?" Tears spilled over her eyelids, streaming down her cheeks. "This isn't real."

"It is, and I'm sorry. I wish there was something I could've done. But he and I, you know, we lived a dangerous life."

"He said he was done with that."

Jack shook his head. "He was working still. Got a job to take out my main support guy, Brandon. Didn't do it and instead got caught up in something pretty big. He did a huge service to us all. Paid the ultimate price, but it wasn't for nothing, sweetie. I promise you that."

Reese remained quiet for several minutes, her gaze aimed downward, her hands folded on the table. Every line in her face seemed new to Jack. It had been a few years, sure, but those years had worn her down. She was still the beautiful woman he'd met a decade before, but there was something else about her now. The years had made her more attractive. An air of confidence surrounded her, even when she was most doubtful.

"You ok?" he asked.

She glanced up, a forced smile on her face. "No, but I will be."

All he could do was nod. He'd lost so many over the years. It was always ok. In the end.

They ordered another round of drinks, eschewing beer for bourbon. The painful memories evaporated, and before he knew it, Reese had grabbed his hand and pulled him out of his chair. They danced to an old Garth Brooks song. Then another. And another.

When Reese finally spoke, her breath was hot against his neck and sent shivers down his spine.

"Can we go back to your room?"

He wanted to tell her no. That she needed to deal with the news in a healthy way. But the fact remained that he loved this woman. And he had been pulled away from her twice already. The chances of it happening a third time were great, so if he had the opportunity, it would be best to take it.

His arm fell, tracing hers along the way, until their fingers intertwined. She looked up at him, eyes wide, tears lingering. He leaned in and kissed her, slow at first, tender. His hand released and his arm wrapped around her lower back, pulling her in closer. They left the bar and made the short walk to the Lewiston Inn, where they found his room and spent the night getting reacquainted.

CHAPTER 10

THE RINGING PHONE ROUSED JACK FROM THE BEST SLEEP HE'D had in two years. Reese's arm was heavy, crossing his chest, her fingers wrapped just under his back. She smelled amazing, something akin to pears and herbs. In those fleeting moments between sleep and wakefulness, driven by the ringing phone, he recalled those moments in Texas where he felt they could have disappeared together and lived a life just the two of them.

Of course, nothing was ever that easy.

And that's why the phone rang now.

Jack reached for his phone, groggy and disoriented. "Hello?"

"Jack, it's Ben. We need to meet. Now." His voice was urgent, cutting through the fog in Jack's mind.

Jack sat up, careful not to wake Reese just yet. "What's going on?"

"I've uncovered something about Hennessey's operations. It's big, Jack. And I've arranged a meeting with an informant who can give us more details."

Jack felt the weight of the situation pressing down on him. Ben's tone left no room for doubt. "Where and when do we meet?"

"There's a secluded spot just outside town. I'll text you the coordinates. Be there in thirty."

Jack hung up, the urgency of the call pulling him into wakefulness. He turned to Reese, brushing a strand of hair from her face. "Reese, wake up."

She stirred, blinking up at him with sleepy eyes. "What is it?"

"We need to meet Ben. He's onto something, and it's urgent."

Reese rubbed her eyes, smiled. "Can it wait?"

"As much as I wish it could, this sounds important."

Reese sat up, the remnants of sleep vanishing from her expression. "All right, let's go."

A few minutes later, they were in the Jeep, on their way out of town. The drive took ten minutes. When they reached the location, Ben was waiting for them. He looked as though he had found a burial site with a dozen missing bodies. They leapt from the Jeep and met him halfway.

"What's the news?" Jack asked.

Ben wasted no time, launching into his briefing. "I found a possible location where Brenda might be held. It's an old warehouse on the outskirts of town. But that's not all. The information I got reveals deeper corruption involving high-level officials. Hennessey's got connections we didn't even know about."

Jack's mind raced as he processed the information. He had a knack for sniffing out a setup, and this sure as hell smelled like one. "Who's the informant? Can we trust this is good information?"

"An insider who used to work for Hennessey. They've agreed to meet us at the warehouse, but we have to move fast. If Hennessey gets wind of this, we're all dead."

Reese looked between Jack and Ben, her expression fierce. "Then let's not waste any more time."

Ben nodded. "I've already scoped out the area. Security is tight, but if we're careful, we can get in and out without raising too much suspicion."

Jack took a deep breath, the gravity of the moment settling over him. "All right. Let's do this."

The morning sun crested over the tree line as they approached the warehouse and cast long shadows across the landscape. The air was thick with tension.

Jack, Ben, and Reese kept a low profile to avoid detection. The early morning light offered limited cover, but they made use of every shadow and obstacle. Jack's senses were on high alert, scanning for any signs of security.

"There," Ben whispered, pointing to a side entrance partially obscured by crates. "We can slip in through there."

They observed the area from a distance, noting the security measures and potential entry points. A few guards patrolled the perimeter, their movements methodical.

Jack motioned for them to wait. "We go in once the guards move to the other side."

The trio moved swiftly and silently, slipping through the side entrance and into the dimly lit interior of the warehouse. They split up, each taking a different section to cover more ground. The warehouse was a maze of old machinery and stacked crates, making it easy to stay hidden but also to get lost.

Jack felt his heart pound in his chest as he navigated the space. He checked room after room, each one empty, but he didn't give up hope. They had to find Brenda and put this thing to rest.

"Jack, over here," Reese's voice crackled softly in his earpiece. He followed her directions, finding her in a small office at the back of the warehouse.

Reese stood beside a filing cabinet, documents spread out on the desk. "Look at this," she said, handing him a map. "It's another location. An old well on the outskirts of town. What would they be looking for there?"

Jack examined the map. "I haven't the foggiest idea. I mean,

I'm not even sure what the hell these people want. What would an old well have to do with anything?"

Reese shrugged. "Another data point, I suppose."

"Let's keep looking around."

They continued searching the office, finding more documents and maps that suggested the well was a crucial location in Hennessey's operations. The evidence was mounting, but Brenda was still out there, possibly in grave danger.

As they were about to leave, a figure emerged from the shadows—a middle-aged man with a nervous expression. He raised his hands in a gesture of peace. "Please, don't hurt me. I've been waiting for you. Ben, we've talked before."

"Who's this?" Jack said.

"He's my guy," Ben said.

"Talk," Jack said.

The informant nodded. "There's a lot at play here. Hennessey has powerful connections."

"Why should we trust you?" Jack asked.

The informant took a deep breath. "Because I work for him. I've seen what he's capable of. And I want out. I want to help bring him down."

"How do you propose you'll do that?" Jack said.

"You want answers," the guy said. "I have them."

"What kind of answers do you have?"

The informant's gaze darted around the room, his nervousness palpable. "I can tell you about Hennessey's operations, his connections, and where Brenda might be. But we need to move quickly. If Hennessey finds out I'm talking to you, we're all dead."

Jack exchanged a glance with Ben and Reese. "Fine. Start talking. What do you know about Brenda?"

The informant nodded, taking a deep breath. "Brenda was taken because she found evidence that could expose Hennessey and his partners. They've been using various fronts for illegal activities. You know, laundering money and bribing officials to get their way."

Reese stepped forward. Her eyes burned with an intensity Jack had never seen. "Do you know where Brenda is now?"

The informant shook his head. "Not exactly. But I have a lead on where they might have moved her recently. There's an abandoned farmhouse about ten miles from here. It's remote, out of the way, and it's a place they've used before to hide people and things they don't want found."

Jack lingered on that last bit for a moment. *Things they don't want found.* What the hell else has gone on around Lewiston?

"Sound like that's where we're headed next," Jack said. "This place could be heavily guarded. We can't afford any mistakes."

They left the warehouse, the morning sun now fully over the trees, casting a harsh light on the path ahead.

As they drove to the farmhouse, the tension in the Jeep was palpable. Jack kept his eyes on the road while his mind raced through potential scenarios and contingencies.

Reese sat beside him, her hand resting on his arm. Something about her touch relaxed him and make him feel as though everything would work out.

"We'll find her, Reese. We have to."

She nodded.

The muscles in his jaw worked triple time as he thought about a woman he'd never met, but now was fully vested in her recovery. "We will."

Ben was in the backseat, double-checking their equipment. "Remember, we go in quietly. We can't afford to alert them to our presence until we're ready."

Jack and Reese agreed, the plan clear in their minds. They drove past the farmhouse and got a feel for the land. Jack drove another quarter mile and pulled off the road. They approached on foot from there to avoid detection. Every step seemed to echo in the silence. There was nothing out there. Just fields and the lone farmhouse. Jack wondered if their own steps could be heard inside. Would they be setting themselves up?

The farmhouse was old and decrepit, its windows boarded up and the surrounding land overgrown with weeds. Despite the abandoned look of the house, they moved cautiously, using the underbrush for cover as they approached.

"There," Ben whispered, pointing to a small side door that looked less fortified than the main entrance. "I bet we can get in through there."

It took a few pulls, but the door gave way. They slipped through the opening and found themselves in a dark, musty corridor. The air was thick with the smell of decay and neglect. They pressed on, moving silently through the hidden corridor.

Jack's senses were on high alert. With every beat of his heart, he felt the movement around him, every creak of the floorboards and distant rustle putting him on edge. They checked room after room, each one empty and abandoned.

The search turned up nothing. Jack ran his hands through his hair, frustrated at the time they'd spent here, uncovering nothing. He turned to the informant. "What gives?"

The man said nothing, staring at the ground.

Jack grabbed the guy by the back of the head, forcing him to look into his eyes. "What are you not telling us?"

The man clenched his eyes shut. Tears spilled over his cheeks.

"Tell me, or so help me, I will end you. Do you understand me? I've killed for less."

The informant shuddered and cried. "I'm sorry. I'm so sorry."

Jack slapped him, pulled his head back, made him look him in the eye again. "What the hell are you sorry for?"

"Upstairs," the informant whispered, his voice barely audible. "They usually keep prisoners in the attic."

With that news, Jack let go of the man. "Come on, let's head up."

They made their way up the narrow staircase, the wood groaning under their weight. The attic was dimly lit, filled with old furniture and discarded items. But in the corner, they found something that made their hearts race.

A small table covered in papers, maps, and photographs. Jack rifled through them, his eyes widening as he recognized some of the locations and faces. One map caught his attention—a detailed layout of another property, with notes scribbled in the margins.

Jack held up the map. "There's something here."

Reese's eyes widened as she looked at the map. "I know this spot. This place is even more remote than the farmhouse. It's a hunting lodge, deep in the woods. Hard to get to, easy to defend."

Ben nodded. "We need to move now. This could be our last chance."

As they made their way back down the stairs, they heard voices approaching the farmhouse. Jack felt hid heart pound against his chest as they hid in the shadows and waited for the voices to pass.

Once the coast was clear, they slipped out the way they came, making their way back to the Jeep.

CHAPTER 11

JACK, REESE, AND BEN ARRIVED AT THE HUNTING LODGE AS the sun's rays crested over the dense forest. The morning dew hung heavy in the air, coating their skin. The building, partially hidden by tall pines, looked desolate and abandoned, but the trio knew better than to let their guard down. The tension in the air was palpable, each step forward heightening their senses.

"Let's scope it out from here." Jack raised his binoculars to his eyes. He scanned the perimeter and took note of the placement of motion sensors and a few well-hidden cameras. "Security's tight. They're definitely hiding something."

Reese knelt beside him, her gaze fixed on the lodge. "We need to be careful. If they're expecting us, we could walk right into a trap."

Ben nodded as he checked his gear one last time. "We'll move in quietly. No unnecessary risks."

The three of them moved cautiously towards the lodge. They used the cover of the trees to avoid detection. Every step was calculated, every rustle of leaves a potential giveaway. They reached the edge of the clearing and paused to assess their final approach.

"There," Ben whispered. He pointed to a small side entrance partially obscured by overgrown bushes. "Looks like our best bet."

They slipped through the underbrush, reaching the door without incident. Jack tested the handle. It was unlocked. He exchanged a quick glance with Reese and Ben before pushing it open. They stepped into a dark corridor.

The interior of the lodge was as decrepit as the exterior. The air was thick with mold and neglect. The trio moved silently, their flashlights cutting through the darkness. The main hallway branched off into several rooms, each filled with old furniture and discarded items.

"Let's split up," Jack whispered. "Ben, you take the basement. Reese, check the first floor. I'll head upstairs."

They nodded in agreement, each disappearing into their assigned areas. Jack made his way up the creaky staircase. It felt like every step was a potential alarm bell. He reached the top and methodically checked each room. Most were empty, filled only with dust and the remnants of past occupants. But as he reached the end of the hall, he found a room that looked different.

Jack pushed open the door to find a small office. Papers were scattered across a desk, and maps covered one wall. He moved closer, his flashlight illuminating the documents. At first glance, they seemed to provide clues—maps of the area, lists of names, dates, and notes scribbled in the margins. But the more Jack examined them, the more he realized something was off. The information was too perfect, too conveniently placed.

It felt like a setup.

"Jack, over here," Reese's voice crackled in his earpiece. He pocketed a few of the papers and headed downstairs. He found her in what looked like an old armory. Weapons lined the walls, and a table in the center held several communication devices.

"Anything?" he asked.

"Nothing that points directly to Brenda." Reese slammed the

device in her hand down on the table. "It's like they were preparing for something, but there's no sign she was ever here."

Jack nodded, his mind racing. "Ben, report," he said into the earpiece.

"Found the basement," Ben's voice crackled back. "But it's empty. Just some scattered papers. Looks like someone cleared out in a hurry."

The weight of the situation pressed down on Jack like a two-ton anvil. "Meet us back in the main hall. We need to regroup."

As they convened in the hallway, Jack spread the documents on the floor. "This feels wrong. It's like they wanted us to find this place."

Reese nodded. "A dead end. But why?"

"Because they're playing us," Jack said. "We need to figure out who's behind this and why they want us chasing our tails."

They were interrupted by the distant sound of vehicles approaching.

Jack's shoulders tensed as he heard the rumble of engines getting closer. "We need to move. Now."

They gathered the documents and stuffed them in Reese's bag, scrambling to find better cover within the lodge. Moments later, the sound of boots hitting the ground echoed through the building. The front door burst open, and a group of armed men stormed inside, their flashlights slicing through the darkness.

"Stay low," Jack whispered.

They ducked behind an old, overturned wooden table. The room was silent aside from their ragged breaths. Flashlight beams sliced through the darkness. Jack peeked over the table. Saw the silhouettes of four men across the room.

The first shots rang out, shattering the silence. Jack, Reese, and Ben returned fire, their tactical training kicking in. The lodge became a chaotic battlefield. Bullets flew and shouts echoed off the walls. After another volley of return fire, the room fell silent again.

Ben eased around the table. "Looks like two are down. One still moving."

Jack nodded and signaled for Reese to cover them. "Let's check on him."

They moved to the man and disarmed him before dragging him behind the table.

"Who are you? Who sent you?" Ben demanded.

The man grimaced in pain but managed a defiant smile. "You're in way over your head, old man."

"Who sent you?" Jack said.

"Marcus Wade," the attacker finally spat out. "He knew you'd come here, Noble."

Jack's thoughts raced back to his last mission with Marcus. They were SIS, working for Frank Skinner. They had been deep in Afghanistan, and a critical decision Jack made had led to Marcus's capture. He had always suspected Marcus blamed him, but he hadn't known the extent of his vendetta. Marcus's grudge had festered over the years, and now it had brought them to this deadly confrontation.

Jack felt a chill run down his spine. "Why?"

The attacker coughed, blood staining his lips. "He has a score to settle with you."

Before Jack could ask any more questions, the wounded man succumbed to his injuries with a final ragged breath.

"We need to get out of here. This place is a dead end."

Jack, Reese, and Ben slipped out through a side entrance, disappearing into the surrounding forest. The sounds of chaos and confusion behind them faded as they put distance between themselves and the lodge. They didn't stop until they were deep in the woods, far from immediate danger.

They found a secluded spot surrounded by thick trees and underbrush, providing them with cover and a chance to catch their breath.

"Everyone okay?" Jack asked.

Ben nodded, though his expression was grim. "A few scrapes, nothing serious."

Reese rubbed her arm where a bullet had grazed her. "I'll be fine. But what now? We're back to square one."

Jack spread out the documents they had taken from the lodge and warehouse. "We need to reassess. There's something here we're missing. Something has to be real, setup or not."

They poured over the papers, searching for any hidden clues. The maps and lists seemed random at first, but patterns began to emerge.

"Look at this." Ben pointed to a series of dates and locations. "These aren't just random places. They're key points in Hennessey's network."

Reese leaned in. "I'm not sure what to make of this. What's the deal with Marcus Wade?"

Jack explained the connection, but the fact the man was in Lewiston made no sense to any of them. Was it by chance? Had he followed Jack here? Or had Reese been placed in the town specifically because Wade was here and there was a chance Jack might show up?

"We need a new strategy," Jack said. "This is bigger than we thought. We need to hit key locations simultaneously. It's the only way to disrupt his operations and create enough chaos to find Brenda."

Ben nodded. "There are three main targets. Hennessey's headquarters, a shipping hub, and what I believe is a safehouse where they might be holding Brenda." He tapped the map. "We'll need to split up to cover more ground. Jack, you and Reese take the safe house. I'll handle the other locations."

"We set up a rendezvous point here." Jack pointed to a spot on the map. "Meet back in six hours. If something goes wrong, we pull back and reassess."

CHAPTER 12

JACK AND REESE DROVE IN SILENCE FOR THE FIRST FEW miles. Jack was still processing the news about Marcus Wade and the implications surrounding it. He no longer had the anonymity he thought. Wade knew him, and that meant Hennessey knew his identity. Did the man have the kind of power that allowed him to do something damaging with the information?

The road stretched out ahead of them, winding through the forest, with the safehouse still some distance away.

Jack finally broke the silence. "You know, I still can't believe you're here, Reese. After all these years."

Reese glanced at him, a small smile playing on her lips. "It's been a wild ride, hasn't it? I never imagined our paths would cross like this again."

"Life has a funny way of bringing people back together." Jack gripped the steering wheel. "I'm just glad we're on the same side."

Reese's smile faded. "I just wish it wasn't under these circumstances. Finding Brenda is all I can think about. Even with the news of my brother. I guess I always figured he'd meet an early end. But Brenda, she's a good woman. Maybe too good. Her crusades grew more dangerous over the past year. And now—"

Jack placed his hand on hers. "We'll find her. We've come too far to back down now."

As they neared the safehouse, they fell silent again. The sun was low in the sky, casting long shadows across the landscape. The house came into view—a nondescript single story that blended into its surroundings.

"Here we are." Jack pulled off the road and parked the car out of sight. They got out, scanning the area for any signs of surveillance or recent activity.

"Looks quiet." Reese glanced all around. Her detective instincts were kicking in. "Almost too quiet."

Jack nodded. "Let's scout the perimeter."

They moved cautiously around the building, noting potential entry points and any possible threats. There didn't appear to be any security in place, at least none they could see.

"Looks clear," Jack whispered. "Let's head in before the light fades completely."

With the sun dipping below the horizon, they approached the house. The shadows deepened, providing them with additional cover. Jack tested the back door and found it locked but not alarmed.

"I'll get us in." Jack pulled out his lock-picking tools. Within moments, the lock clicked open, and they slipped inside, their movements silent and deliberate.

The interior was dimly lit by the fading light filtering through the dirty windows. They moved through the darkened rooms, their flashlights casting beams of light that revealed the disarray within.

The place was a mess. Overturned furniture, scattered papers, and broken items littered the floor. Either someone had left in a hurry or the place had been ransacked. If it was the latter, then who had done it? What kind of enemies did Hennessey have?

"Doesn't look promising." Reese's flashlight swept over the chaos.

"How much do you know about Hennessey?"

She shrugged. "Just what Brenda said."

"Enemies?"

"I imagine he's pissed off his share of politicians and whatnot."

"So maybe there is something in this chaos." Jack scanned the room for any clues. "Let's keep looking."

They moved deeper into the house, stepping over broken glass and debris. The air was thick with dust, and every creak of the floorboards sounded like a gunshot in the silence.

Reese's flashlight caught a glint of something metallic half-buried under a pile of papers. She knelt down and sifted through the mess, found an old, battered briefcase. She opened it, revealing a disorganized pile of documents, some of which looked relatively recent.

"Jack, over here," she called softly, holding up a sheet of paper.

Jack joined her and peered at the paper she had found. It was an email printout, addressed to someone named Carl. The subject line read "Project Updates," and the body of the email contained a series of coded messages and coordinates.

"Carl," Jack muttered. "That's Hennessey's name."

Reese nodded. "This could be a lead. Look at the sender's email address."

Jack glanced at the top of the email: wade.marcus21@gmail.-com. His jaw clenched. "Marcus Wade. He's deeper into this than we thought."

Reese's eyes narrowed. "There's a phone number at the bottom. We can use this later to trace more information."

Jack took a photo of the email with his phone. "Let's keep moving. There has to be more."

They continued searching the rooms, their flashlights revealing more signs of a hurried departure. Jack's beam landed on a small, leather-bound notebook partially hidden under a couch cushion. He flipped through it, finding pages filled with hastily scribbled notes and diagrams.

"Check this out." He tossed the notebook to Reese.

She skimmed through the pages, her brow furrowing. "Looks like a lot of plans and financial records. Some of these notes mention a 'main event.'"

"Whatever that means, it's not good. We need to find out more."

Reese flipped to the last few pages and found an entry that stood out. "Jack, listen to this: 'Safe house compromised. Moving assets to secondary location. Ensure all records are transferred. Destroy remaining evidence.'"

Jack's eyes widened. "So they knew this place was blown. They must have moved everything important."

"Secondary location," Reese repeated, scanning the room. "There might be something here that tells us where that is."

Jack moved to the desk in the corner of the room. He rifled through the drawers, coming across various office supplies and more documents. One drawer was locked. He pulled out his tools again and picked the lock. Inside, he found a small key and a slip of paper with an address scribbled on it.

"This could be it," Jack said, holding up the key and the paper. "Let's check the basement. There might be something down there that confirms this is where they moved."

They headed back to the locked door Reese had found earlier. Jack used the key to unlock it, and they descended the creaky stairs into the basement.

The basement was a stark contrast to the chaos upstairs. It was clean and organized, with a makeshift office setup. Jack took note of the computer on the desk, stacks of files, and a map on the wall with various locations marked. He recognized them from files they had found at the previous locations.

"Looks like we hit the jackpot." Jack moved towards the desk.

Reese examined the files, her flashlight illuminating the neatly stacked papers. "These are detailed records of Hennessey's operations. Financial transactions, project plans, even some personnel files."

Jack clicked the mouse and the computer screen cast a pale glow in the dim basement. "This could have everything we need." He opened folders and scanned documents. "Emails, financial records, schedules. This is a goldmine."

Reese's flashlight beam landed on a series of photographs pinned to the wall. She moved closer, her breath catching in her throat. "Jack, look at this."

Jack joined her, his eyes widening as he saw photographs of Brenda. Some showed her in what looked like an interrogation room, while others were in various locations that matched the ones on the map.

"She was here," Reese said. "But where is she now? And these photos of her in the other places, was that surveillance? Or did they drag her there?"

"Starting to think your friend was deeper in this than you might have known."

Reese nodded. "I'm coming to that same conclusion."

"What's that say about Ben?"

"He's probably deeper in this than he let you know."

Jack's eyes narrowed as he continued to scan the room. "Let's see if we can find out." He moved to the other desk, opened drawers and rifled through their contents. His hand brushed against something solid, and he pulled out a hidden drawer. Inside was a USB drive. He held up the drive. "We can analyze it later. Let's keep searching."

As they were about to leave, Reese's phone rang, the sound jarring in the silent basement. She looked at the screen—an unknown number. "I should answer this."

Her face went pale as she listened.

"What? Are you sure?" Her voice trembled. She ended the call and looked at Jack, her eyes wide with shock. "Brenda's been found."

Jack's heart skipped a beat. "What? Where?"

Reese swallowed hard. "They found her body in a well on a remote property."

The weight of the news hit them hard. Jack felt a mix of anger and grief swell within him. "We need to see the body. We need to know what happened."

Reese slammed into him, her arms wrapped around his shoulders. She pulled him in tight as she sobbed on his chest. After a moment, she pulled away.

"Sorry," she said.

"Don't be," he said. "Come on, let's go. We've found everything we could." Before they could move, he noticed a thin wisp of smoke curling up from the far corner of the basement. "Reese, we need to get out of here. Now."

Reese turned to see the smoke spreading rapidly. "What's going on?"

"It's a fire. They're destroying the place. We need to move!"

PART 2

CHAPTER 13

THE BASEMENT FILLED WITH SMOKE. THE ACRID SCENT
filled their lungs as they grabbed the USB drive and important
documents they had found. The situation was deteriorating
rapidly.

"We need to move, now!" Jack shouted.

Reese nodded. They navigated through the thickening smoke.
Jack led the way with his flashlight cutting through the haze. At
the top of the stairs, he felt the door and knob. Both were warm,
but not burning to the touch. He threw his shoulder into the door
as he opened it. Smoke billowed in from the main floor. It was
impossible to see anything even a foot away. He dropped to his
knees and lowered his chest to the ground. The smoke was thinner
here and he could make out the front door.

He led Reese through the increasingly dangerous environment.

Before they could reach the main door, it erupted into flames.
Jack cursed under his breath, scanning for another exit. "This
way!" he yelled, pointing to a window.

Flames approached. They licked at the wall, closing in on the
new escape point. Jack raced the fire and reached the window.

The heat was intense. Sweat coated his entire body, stung his eyes. He rose into the thick cloud of dark smoke. His hands traced the glass, found the latch. It didn't budge. He pulled his pistol out and broke the window, top to bottom. He slid the barrel around the edges, freeing as much of the razor sharp remains as possible. He set the folders he carried along the bottom to offer additional protection.

Reese squeezed through the opening first, Jack following close behind. They landed in the backyard and scrambled to get away from the house. The cool night air was a stark contrast to the inferno raging behind them. The structure began to collapse, the sound of breaking wood and shattering glass filling the air.

"Come on, we need to get farther away!" Jack pulled Reese up from the ground. They sprinted to a safer distance, their breaths ragged from the exertion and smoke inhalation.

Once they reached a secure spot, they collapsed to the ground and turned to watch the house burn. The flames illuminated the night, casting eerie shadows across the trees. Jack could feel his heart pounding in his chest, adrenaline still coursing through his veins.

Reese leaned against a tree, her eyes wide with shock and relief. She coughed hard. "That was too close."

Jack wiped sweat and soot from his forehead. "But we made it out. I lost the folders though."

Reese held up the USB drive, the small object now their life-line in uncovering the truth. "We've got this. Let's find Ben. We need to regroup and figure out our next move."

Jack nodded, his mind already shifting to their next steps.

JACK AND REESE SPED THROUGH THE BACKROADS. Adrenaline still coursed through his veins. Once it wore off, the pain of their scrapes, cuts and burns would hit. The darkness around them felt oppressive, and every shadow seemed like a potential threat. They had to reach Ben quickly and regroup.

Reese checked the rearview mirror for the hundredth time, her eyes darting between the road ahead and the side mirrors. "I don't think we're being followed, but we can't be too careful."

Jack nodded, his grip on the steering wheel tight. "We'll take a few more turns, just to be sure."

They drove in silence. Each turn brought them closer to the prearranged meeting point. Finally, they reached a secluded clearing deep in the woods. Ben's car was already there, parked in the shadows.

Jack parked the Jeep and killed the engine. They stepped out and scanned the area one last time before approaching Ben.

Ben emerged from the darkness, his face covered with concern. "What the hell happened?"

Jack and Reese updated him on the fire, the discovery of Brenda's body, and the potential significance of the information they had retrieved.

Ben's eyes narrowed as he listened and processed the news. "Ah, Brenda. I held out hope she was alive, but I can't say this is unexpected. I've known for a while that Hennessey is a terrible man." He tipped his head back and stared up at the sky. "This fire, it wasn't an accident. Someone knew we were close and they wanted to destroy any evidence."

Jack nodded. "That's what we figured. They could've been tipped off by your informant. Or the guys shooting at us at the lodge."

Reese held up the USB drive. "We still have this. It might give us some answers."

Ben glanced at the small device, his expression grim. "We need to be careful. If they're willing to kill Brenda and burn down a safehouse, they won't stop at anything."

"We need to find a secure location to analyze this drive. Somewhere we won't be interrupted."

Ben nodded. "I have a place in mind. It's off the grid, secure, and has everything we need."

They piled into their vehicles and drove deeper into the woods. The tension in the air was palpable, each of them lost in their thoughts. The fire had been a close call, but they had to keep moving forward.

As they reached Ben's hideout, a small cabin hidden among the trees, they took a moment to catch their breath.

Jack looked at Reese and Ben. "Let's see what's on this drive and figure out our next move."

They sat around a small table in the cabin. The USB drive lay in the center, the small object holding potentially crucial information. Ben booted up a laptop and plugged the drive in, a mix of anticipation and dread filling the room.

"We'll need a password," Ben said as he navigated through the folders. He tried a few combinations based on what they knew about Hennessey and Brenda but had no success.

"We should try to think like Hennessey or whoever set this up," Reese said. "What kind of password would they use?"

Ben nodded. "Hennessey is meticulous. It's likely something personal yet complex."

Reese leaned in. Her fingernails tapped the table. "We could try significant dates, names, or phrases he might use."

Ben opened a browser tab and typed in log-in credentials to a law enforcement database. He looked up Brenda's information on the site, then typed in her name and birthday, then a few more potential phrases related to Hennessey's operations. The screen flashed red with each failed attempt.

"Damn, it's locked tight," he muttered. "We'll need more clues to crack this."

Reese thought for a moment, then snapped her fingers. "What

about the coded messages we found at the lodge? There might be something in those notes."

They sifted through the documents they had taken from the burning house, focusing on any cryptic notes or unusual patterns. Ben cross-referenced those with the USB, but nothing worked.

"Could we have overlooked something?" Jack said. "There must be a way to figure this out."

Reese held up a finger. "Wait, Brenda mentioned a personal connection with Hennessey. Something about his daughter. What if it's related to her?"

Ben found a record for Hennessey's daughter and typed in her name followed by her birthdate. The screen flashed green, and they were in.

"Got it!" Ben said.

They sifted through the files. The contents of the USB drive were extensive, including financial records, emails, and detailed plans. It was clear Hennessey's operations were more complex and far-reaching than they had anticipated. And the money was coming in from a number of sources, several criminal.

"This is huge." Reese's voice was filled with awe and dread. "We need to go through all of this, but first, we gotta see Brenda's body and confirm what we've been told."

"Agreed," Jack said. "Let's gather what we need and get to the property."

They packed their gear, ensuring they had everything necessary for both an investigation and any potential confrontation. Weapons, first aid supplies, and communication devices were double-checked and loaded into their vehicles.

The drive to the property where Brenda's body had been discovered was tense. The silence between them was heavy with the weight of their discoveries. Jack's thoughts raced as he considered what they might find and how they would proceed from there.

"We need to be ready for anything," Reese said, breaking the silence. "If Hennessey's people are there, I don't think they're just gonna welcome us."

Jack nodded, his eyes focused on the road ahead. "We'll stay sharp. The moment we see anything suspicious, we pull back and reassess. We can't afford to take unnecessary risks."

As they neared the property, the landscape became more remote and foreboding. Tall trees lined the narrow road, their branches casting long shadows in the moonlight. Jack slowed the car as he studied the surroundings for any signs of movement.

"There it is." Reese pointed to a dilapidated farmhouse in the distance. "That's where they found her."

Jack parked the car a safe distance away, and they continued on foot. The air was thick with anticipation, every sound magnified in the stillness. They approached the property cautiously, their senses on high alert.

"Let's go," Jack said.

CHAPTER 14

THEY APPROACHED THE PERIMETER OF THE SCENE, TAKING IN the grim reality of the situation. The well was at the center of the activity, its edges illuminated by bright floodlights. Jack, Reese, and Ben watched as officers pulled Brenda's body from the well. Reese turned toward Jack and wrapped her arms around him. He pulled her in, feeling her sorrow as she shook.

The expressions on the faces of the emergency personnel were solemn. This wasn't an everyday occurrence in the small town, and not something they were used to dealing with.

As they neared the perimeter, a police officer stepped forward to intercept them. "Stop there. This is an active crime scene. Who are you?"

Ben stepped into the light and showed his identification. "We're here to help. We have information that could be crucial to this case."

The officer scrutinized their IDs, then radioed his superior. Moments later, a detective approached them.

"Ben. Didn't expect to see you here."

Ben held out his hand. "Harris, good to see you. This is Jack, and you know Tanya."

Jack met the detective's gaze. "We've been investigating Brenda's disappearance. We have reason to believe there's more to this than meets the eye."

Harris nodded, weighing his options. "All right, but tread carefully. We're all on edge here. What have you got?"

They moved closer to the well, careful not to disturb the ongoing work. They observed the scene, noting the haphazard way the officers handled Brenda's body.

Reese scanned the surroundings, taking in every detail. "Something doesn't feel right about this."

Ben's expression was grim. "We need to look at the well and the surrounding area. There might be clues they've missed."

With Detective Harris's reluctant permission, they approached the well. Jack peered inside, noting the depth and the condition of the walls. "This wasn't a random dump site. Someone wanted her to be found eventually."

Reese nodded. "We need to figure out who and why."

Detective Harris kept a watchful eye on them, his skepticism lingering despite his willingness to allow them access to the scene. Perhaps he knew he was outmatched by the case.

The scene was bathed in an eerie glow from the floodlights. Long shadows danced on the ground. The officers laid Brenda's body on a stretcher, their movements respectful and precise.

"Let's take a closer look," Jack said.

Reese closed her eyes and took a deep breath. She exhaled and nodded her readiness. They approached the body. Jack crouched down and examined Brenda's face and hands. His trained eye picked up on subtle details others might miss.

"There are bruises on her wrists." Jack felt anger welling up at the thought of what Brenda's final minutes must've been like. "She was restrained."

Reese's gaze moved to Brenda's clothing. "Look at her shoes.

There's dirt on them, but it's not from around here. It's red. This ground is almost black. She was moved."

"Someone wanted her found, but only after they were done with her."

Reese's jaw tightened. "She didn't deserve this. We need to find out who did this and make them pay."

As they continued their examination, Jack noticed something else. "There's blood under her nails. She fought back."

Ben joined them. "Any idea who?"

Jack shook his head. "No clues that point to that. But we're going to find out."

Detective Harris stepped closer, his curiosity piqued despite himself. "Find anything useful?"

Jack stood up, faced Harris. "She was restrained, moved post-mortem, and she fought back at some point. This wasn't just a murder. It was a message."

Harris's eyes narrowed as he dragged a hand across his stubble. "A message to who?"

"To anyone who gets too close to the truth."

Reese looked around the scene. "We need to talk to everyone who knew Brenda, everyone she worked with. Someone has to know something."

Jack nodded. "And we need to dig deeper into Hennessey's operations."

"All right." Harris paused a beat as he stared down at the corpse. "I'll get you access to what we have so far. But be careful. We don't know who we're dealing with."

"Why are you so willing to help?" Reese asked.

Harris attempted a smile, but it didn't have any effect. "Well, first off, I've known Ben my whole life, know the kind of man he is and what kind of experience he has. Two, I don't want the State Police to take over. It's only a matter of time until they do."

"What aren't you telling us?" Jack asked.

Detective Harris gestured for them to follow him to a more private area away from the other officers. "I need to know everything you've found out so far."

Jack glanced at Reese and Ben before starting. "We've been looking into Hennessey's operations. Brenda was onto something big. We found documents and a USB drive at a safe house. It looks like Hennessey has been involved in a lot of illegal activities, using his business as a front. I'd guess Brenda discovered enough to put her in serious danger."

Harris took out a notebook and jotted down notes. "Anything specific that ties Hennessey directly to her murder?"

Reese shook her head. "Not yet. But we believe the same people who set the fire at the safehouse are behind this, and they are tied to Hennessey. It's too much of a coincidence."

Harris paused, flipping through his notes. "We've been looking into Brenda's ex-boyfriend, Mark Cundiff. He's been a person of interest for a while. History of violence, past threats against Brenda. Do you know anything about him?"

Jack and Reese exchanged a glance. He didn't want to reveal too much to Harris. Reese had a connection with Brenda and was familiar with Cundiff.

"Heard about him," Jack said. "But we haven't had the chance to dig deep. If he's involved, he might have connections to Hennessey. Or perhaps he was played, used by Hennessey."

"You think Hennessey might've manipulated him, got him to take out Brenda?"

"Possible."

Harris took a moment before continuing. He tapped his pen against his notebook. "Cundiff's been laying low, but we've had our eyes on him. He's definitely a person of interest, even more so now."

Reese clenched her fists. "If Mark is involved, we need to find him. He could be the missing link in all of this. What if he knows Hennessey's plans? Or what Brenda was close to cracking?"

Ben placed a reassuring hand on Reese's shoulder. "We'll find him. But we need to be smart about this. Rushing in could get us killed."

Harris looked at each of them. "I'll help as much as I can, but we need to keep this quiet. If word gets out, it could jeopardize the entire investigation."

Jack took a deep breath as his mind raced ahead. "We'll split up. Reese, you focus on gathering more information about Mark Cundiff. Talk to anyone who knew him and Brenda. Don't go near him, though. We'll handle that as a team. Ben and I will look into other connections Brenda had. Someone has to know something that can help us."

"I'll start with Brenda's close friends. They're most likely to know Mark as well. Maybe they've noticed something off about him recently."

Ben glanced at Jack. "We should also go through the information on the USB drive. There might be something we missed that can point us in the right direction."

As they prepared to leave, Jack pulled Reese aside. "We're going to find out who did this, Reese. Brenda deserves justice."

Reese's eyes filled with tears. She wiped them away. "I know. I'm not stopping until everyone is brought to justice."

CHAPTER 15

AFTER A FEW HOURS OF SLEEP, JACK AND REESE SAT IN THE dimly lit cabin, the USB drive plugged into Ben's laptop on the table between them. The glow from the screen cast shadows on their faces as they sifted through the documents they had retrieved. The tension in the air was palpable.

"We need to dig deeper into Cundiff's background," Jack said. "There has to be something that ties him to Brenda's death aside from the obvious."

"I'll start with his criminal record. Let's see what we're dealing with."

They worked in silence for a few minutes, each of them absorbed in their task. Reese pulled up Mark's criminal record. Her brows furrowed as she read through the list of offenses. "Assault, battery, restraining orders... This guy has more of a history of violence than I was aware of."

Jack leaned over to look at the screen. "And look at this. He was arrested for stalking his ex-girlfriend before Brenda. It's a pattern." Jack clicked on another document, his eyes narrowing as he read. "He was obsessed with Brenda. Threatened her multiple times when she tried to break things off."

Reese's jaw tightened. "She only mentioned him threatening her once. I had no idea it was this bad. This guy is dangerous. And if he was willing to go that far with Brenda, who knows what else he's capable of?"

Jack closed the laptop and stood up. He walked over the window, peeled the curtains back. The sun was rising. "We need to talk to Brenda's friends. They might have noticed something off about Mark recently."

Reese grabbed her jacket and followed him to the door. "Let's start with Sarah. That's her best friend since childhood. She's most likely to know if something was going on."

"I spoke with her the other day. Maybe she'll have more to say now."

They drove to Sarah's house. Jack knocked on the door, and a moment later, Sarah answered, her eyes red from crying.

"Jack, Tanya," she said, her voice trembling. "Come in."

They followed her into the living room and sat down. "Sarah, we're so sorry for your loss," Reese began. "We need to ask you a few questions about Brenda and Mark Cundiff. It's important."

Sarah nodded, her eyes welling up with tears. "I'll do anything to help. Brenda was my best friend."

"Think about everything she ever told you," Jack said. "Anything you might have forgotten last time I visited you."

Reese leaned forward. "Did Brenda ever mention any recent interactions with Mark? Anything that might indicate he was threatening her?"

Sarah wiped her eyes and took a deep breath. "Brenda told me Mark had been following her more frequently. She was scared. He sent her threatening messages, saying she couldn't escape him. She tried to get a restraining order, but it didn't stop him."

Jack exchanged a glance with Reese. "Did Brenda ever mention anything about Mark being involved with someone else? Maybe someone who might have helped him?"

Sarah shook her head. "No, she always said Mark acted alone. But she did mention seeing him talking to some shady characters around town. She thought he might be getting involved in something dangerous. Said she spotted them near her house, too."

Jack and Reese exchanged a look, the implications of Sarah's words settling heavily between them.

"Shady characters?" Reese said. "Did she ever describe them or mention any names?"

Sarah hesitated a moment as she searched the ceiling for answers. "She said they were well-dressed, like businessmen, but there was something off about them. She thought one of them looked familiar, like she'd seen him around town before."

Jack leaned in. "Did she ever mention the name Hennessey?"

Sarah's eyes widened. "Yes, she did. A few times, actually. And she recently told me she saw Mark talking to a man who looked like Hennessey outside a bar. She thought it was strange, but she didn't think much of it at the time."

Could that be the link they were looking for? Was it enough that Brenda had confided to Sarah that she'd seen two men who might want her dead?

"What else did she tell you about Hennessey?" Jack asked.

"Not too much. I know he's involved in some of the things Brenda was crusading against." She leaned back and rubbed her eyes. "Do you think he's involved in her disappearance and murder?"

"That's what we're trying to figure out," Reese said. "Is there anything else you can recall?"

Sarah shook her head. "I'm just in such a state of shock. I can't believe she's gone."

Jack offered her his hand. "Sarah, thank you. You've been incredibly helpful. We'll get to the bottom of this."

Sarah wiped away her tears. "Please, find out who did this to Brenda. She didn't deserve any of this."

Back in the car, Reese looked over at Jack. "If we can prove Hennessey and Mark are connected, we can blow this whole thing wide open."

"Let's get back to the cabin. We need to go through the information on the USB again."

Back at the cabin, Jack and Reese pieced together the information they had gathered. Jack spread out the documents on the table. The dots were there, they just had to connect them.

"Mark's history of violence, his obsession with Brenda, the threats, it all fits. But we need more. We need to find a direct link between Mark and Hennessey."

Reese picked up a photo of Brenda and stared at it. Her eyes teared up. "Brenda knew something. She was close to uncovering the truth, and it got her killed."

Jack placed a reassuring hand on her shoulder. "I think we need a one on one with Mark Cundiff soon."

CHAPTER 16

Jack and Reese sat in the car outside Mark Cundiff's rundown apartment. The parking lot was full of older vehicles, all of which were dented and dinged. The sunlight did little to help the appearance of the dilapidated building. They had been watching for a while, seen Mark enter and exit his apartment, never going far. The time had come to confront him.

"Are you ready for this?" Reese asked, her eyes fixed on the entrance to Mark's apartment.

Jack nodded. "He's likely to be defensive and might try to bolt. Or worse."

They stepped out of the car and made their way to Mark's unit. The apartment complex was in a state of disrepair, with peeling paint and overgrown weeds. They climbed the creaky stairs to the second floor and found Mark's door. Jack knocked firmly.

A moment later, the door swung open, and Mark stood before them, his eyes narrowing as he recognized Reese. "What do you want?"

"We need to talk," Jack said. "It's about Brenda."

Mark's face contorted with anger. "I've already told the cops everything I know. I didn't have anything to do with her disappearance or death."

"We're not here to accuse you," Reese said. "We just want to hear your side of the story. Can we come in?"

"You're not cops," he said. "Why should I talk to you?"

"You're right," Jack said. "We're not. And that means we don't have to play by their rules. Talk to us now, or I'll make you talk to us later."

Mark hesitated, his eyes darting between them. Finally, he stepped aside and allowed them to enter. The apartment was a mess, with empty beer cans and dirty clothes strewn about. The air was thick with the smell of stale cigarettes.

"Make it quick," Mark muttered, slumping into a worn-out chair. "I've got nothing to say to you."

Jack and Reese took seats across from him. "We know about your history with Brenda," Jack said. "We know about the threats, the stalking. We also know she saw you talking to some dangerous people. We need to understand your relationship with her and what you know about these men."

Mark clenched his jaw and exhaled loudly. "I loved Brenda, okay? But she didn't want anything to do with me after we broke up. She got that restraining order. After that, I stayed away. I only followed her to make sure she was safe. I never hurt her."

"Why did you feel you needed to make sure she was safe?" Reese asked.

"Because of things," Mark said.

Reese leaned forward. "What about Hennessey? Brenda saw you talking to him. What was that about?"

Mark's face paled slightly, but he quickly regained his composure. "I don't know what you're talking about. I don't know any Hennessey."

"Don't lie to us," Jack said. "We have witnesses who saw you with him. We know Brenda was onto something big, something that got her killed. You need to tell us what you know."

Mark shifted in his chair, his eyes darting around the room. "I told you, I don't know anything. I'm just a guy trying to get by."

Reese stood and paced to the front door and back. "We're not leaving until you give us something. If you're innocent, you have nothing to fear. But if you're hiding something, now's the time to come clean."

Mark's hands clenched into fists. His knuckles turned white. "Look, all right, I talked to some guys. They offered me money to keep tabs on Brenda, to find out what she knew."

"That's how you kept her safe?" Jack said.

"I swear I didn't know it would get her killed!"

Jack's eyes locked onto Mark's. "Who were they? Names."

"I don't know their real names." Mark's voice was trembling and tears welled in his eyes. Were they for Brenda, or was he scared he was next? "They called themselves 'associates' of Hennessey. That's all I know. They paid me, and I did what they asked. But I didn't hurt Brenda." He lowered his head and stared down at his hands. "I didn't know they would."

Reese glanced at Jack. "You're coming with us, Mark. We're going to get to the bottom of this, and you're going to help us."

Mark's shoulders slumped in defeat. "Fine. But I'm telling you, I didn't kill her."

"Let's go," Jack said, guiding Mark out of the apartment. They made their way back to the car, keeping a close eye on their surroundings.

As they drove back to the cabin, tense silence filled the car. Jack kept glancing at Mark through the rearview mirror. The man seemed to grow more nervous by the second.

"Why are you so jumpy?" Jack said.

Mark stared out the window. "I'm not jumpy. I just–I didn't want any of this. I didn't sign up for murder."

"You said these men approached you," Reese said. "Why would they pick you to spy on Brenda?"

Mark shrugged, his voice shaking. "I don't know. Maybe because I was close to her once. Because I knew her routines, her habits."

Jack pressed on. "You said they paid you. How much? And how often?"

Mark hesitated, then muttered, "A couple thousand. Every few weeks."

Reese's instincts kicked in. "What did they expect in return for that kind of money?"

"Information," Mark said. "They wanted to know where she went, who she talked to. I mean, these guys were more obsessed with her movements than me."

Jack's grip on the steering wheel tightened. "And you never questioned why? Never thought about what they might do with that information?"

"I swear, I didn't think they'd kill her. I thought they were just, I don't know, business rivals or something."

"She's a teacher. What kind of business rivals would she have?"

"You know, all that eco-warrior shit she's involved with." Mark clenched his eyes. "Was involved with."

Reese exchanged a look with Jack. "This isn't adding up. We're missing something."

When they arrived at the cabin, Ben was waiting outside. He took one look at Mark and nodded. "Get inside. We need to talk."

They all filed into the cabin, and Ben closed the door behind them. The atmosphere was tense, the weight of their discoveries hanging heavy in the air. Ben gestured for everyone to sit down.

"I've been going through the USB drive while you were out," Ben said. "There's something you all need to see."

He walked over to the laptop and pulled up a folder on the screen. "These are financial transactions. Large sums of money being moved between shell companies. And look here," he pointed to a document, "payments made to a 'Mark C.'"

Mark's face went slack. "I didn't know they kept records."

"Of course they did," Reese said. "They need to keep their associates in line."

Ben continued. "There's more. I found communication logs—emails and messages between Hennessey and his associates. They discuss Brenda's investigation and how close she was getting to uncovering their operations. Hennessey ordered her to be 'dealt with.'"

Jack's expression darkened. "So it's confirmed. Hennessey is behind this."

Reese turned to Mark. "Do you see now? They were using you. You were never safe."

Mark buried his face in his hands. "I didn't know. I thought I was just spying. I didn't think they'd kill her."

Ben crossed his arms, his gaze fixed on Mark. "We need everything you know about these men. Names, places they meet, anything that can help us take them down."

Mark nodded, still shaking. "I'll tell you everything. There's a warehouse on the outskirts of town. That's where they meet sometimes. And there's a guy named Marcus. He's one of Hennessey's top men."

Jack stood up. "We need to act fast. We'll go to the warehouse, see what we can find. Ben, stay here with Mark. Keep him safe."

Ben nodded. "Got it. Be careful out there. Hennessey's men won't hesitate to kill if they're cornered."

CHAPTER 17

JACK AND REESE DROVE IN SILENCE AS THEY APPROACHED THE edge of town. The landscape became more industrial, the buildings larger and more spread out. Their destination, a seemingly abandoned warehouse, loomed in the distance. Jack parked the car a safe distance away, behind a line of trees that offered some cover.

"Are you ready for this?" Jack asked.

"We have to be. If Mark is right, this might our best chance to gather solid evidence against Hennessey."

They exited the car and moved through the woods. The warehouse was surrounded by a tall chain-link fence topped with barbed wire, but Jack spotted a potential weak point.

"Over there." He pointed to a section of the fence that looked less secure.

Reese nodded, and they moved toward the spot, staying low to avoid detection. Jack pulled out a pair of wire cutters from his bag and snipped through the links, creating an opening large enough for them to slip through.

Once inside the perimeter, they paused to assess their surroundings. The warehouse was a massive structure, with a few small windows high up on the walls and a single large entrance at the front. The area was quiet, the only sound being the distant hum of machinery from a nearby factory.

"Let's stick to the shadows," Jack said. "We don't know what security is like here."

They moved cautiously, staying close to the walls and using the sparse cover to their advantage. As they reached the side of the warehouse, Jack checked a door. It was locked, but not heavily secured. He pulled out a set of lock-picking tools and got to work. Within moments, the lock clicked open.

"After you," Jack whispered, pushing the door open slightly.

Reese slipped inside first, followed closely by Jack. The interior of the warehouse was dimly lit, with only a few overhead lights creating pools of light on the floor. The air was thick with dust and the faint smell of oil. Given the large doors on either end, Jack figured they might repair farm equipment here. They moved through the large open space, their footsteps echoing softly on the concrete floor.

They began their search, moving through the rows of shelves and storage crates. Jack's flashlight beam cut through the darkness. There were stacks of old machinery and boxes labeled with cryptic codes.

"Look over here." Reese pointed to a small office space enclosed by glass walls at the far end of the warehouse.

They approached the office, looking inside to ensure it was empty. The door was unlocked. They stepped inside. The office was cluttered with papers, ledgers, and a few old filing cabinets.

"This looks promising," Jack said. "Start with the desk."

They sifted through the documents, searching for anything that could link Hennessey to his illegal activities. Reese opened a drawer and pulled out a ledger. She flipped through the pages.

"Jack, look at this. These are financial records. Large sums of money being moved around, payments to shell companies."

Jack leaned over her shoulder. "This is exactly what we need. If we can tie these transactions back to Hennessey, along with the others Ben found, we can build a solid case."

He continued searching, opening another drawer and finding a stack of correspondence. As he scanned the letters and memos, one name stood out: Marcus Wade.

"Reese, check this out." He handed her a letter. "It's from Marcus Wade. He's deeply involved in this."

Reese's eyes widened as she read the letter. "This is huge. We need to take all of this with us."

They quickly gathered the most incriminating documents and stuffed them into their bags. As they finished their search, a noise outside the office caught Jack's attention. He held up a hand, signaling Reese to be silent. They listened intently, hearing the faint sound of voices and footsteps approaching.

"We need to move," Jack whispered. "Now."

They slipped out of the office, moving quickly but quietly through the back of warehouse. The voices grew louder, and they could hear the murmur of a conversation. Jack and Reese ducked behind a stack of crates. He peered around the corner to see a group of Hennessey's men entering the warehouse.

The men were close enough Jack and Reese could hear their discussion. Problem was, it was mid-conversation, and key details had been missed. Noble picked up on one thing in particular though. One of the guys said everyone will find out in forty-eight hours. The men continued to the office. The door shut behind them and the warehouse was silent again.

"You catch that?" he said. "Forty-eight hours."

Reese nodded. "We need to get out of here before they find us."

Jack led the way back to the side door they had entered through. They slipped outside, the cool air a welcome relief from the stale atmosphere inside. They moved back to the fence and slipped through the opening they had created earlier.

Once they were a safe distance away, Jack stopped to catch his breath. "I think we've got what we need."

"Now we just need to figure out our next move."

As they headed back to the car, Jack's phone buzzed with a new message. He glanced at the screen. Ice flowed through his veins as he read the message.

I know what you're up to, Noble. You can't hide from me.

Marcus Wade. Finally.

Jack's grip tightened on the phone as memories of their last mission together flooded back. The betrayal, the anger, the unresolved tension between them.

"We need to talk." Jack showed Reese the message.

"What's this guy capable of?" she asked.

"Everything I am. Maybe more."

Jack's hands were steady as he drove back to the cabin, his mind anything but calm. The message from Marcus had stirred up memories he'd tried to bury for years. Reese, sensing his unease, watched him closely.

"What happened between you and Marcus?" Reese asked, breaking the silence.

Jack took a deep breath, his knuckles white against the steering wheel. "It was our last mission together, in Afghanistan. We were working for a man named Frank Skinner. We were deep in enemy territory. Our task was to extract a high-value target from a fortified compound. Everything went according to plan, until it didn't."

"What went wrong?"

Jack's gaze was distant, his voice tinged with regret. "We were ambushed. Someone had tipped off the enemy. It was chaos. We managed to fight our way out, but Marcus got separated from the team. He was captured."

"And you went back for him?" Reese asked.

Jack's jaw tightened. "Yeah. Wasn't easy. I had to pull a lot of strings, risk my career and a few men's lives to mount a rescue operation. We got him out, but he wasn't the same after that. He'd been tortured, broken in ways that can't be fixed."

"And he blames you for that?"

Jack nodded. "He thinks I didn't come for him fast enough, that I left him to suffer. No matter what I did to save him, it wasn't enough in his eyes. He held a grudge. I'm seeing now that it festered over the years."

Reese was silent for a moment as she soaked in the story. "Do you think he could've killed Brenda?"

"Absolutely." Jack's grip on the steering wheel tightened. "Marcus has always been driven by anger and revenge. If he thinks Brenda was a threat to his operations, he wouldn't hesitate."

They drove in silence until they reached the cabin.

When they arrived, Ben briefed them on what he had found linking Mark Cundiff to Hennessey's operations. Mark sat at the table. He looked defeated. It didn't take much to get him to provide the details he had omitted about his interactions with Hennessey's men. The connection was confirmed.

As they discussed their next move, Jack's mind drifted back to Marcus. He knew dealing with Marcus would require more than just tactical planning. It would mean confronting the ghosts of his past.

Jack brought himself back to the present. "We'll go back to town, see what we can find. Ben, stay here with Mark. Keep him safe."

Ben nodded. "Got it. Be careful out there. We've stirred up a hornet's nest, and I'm certain there are goons all over town looking for us."

Jack and Reese prepared to leave, but before they stepped out the door, Reese placed a hand on Jack's arm. "We'll get through this, Jack. We've come this far, and we won't let the past stop us."

Jack looked into her eyes and nodded. "Let's finish this."

But the incoming call to Jack's cell phone would change their plans.

CHAPTER 18

"Hello, Jack. Been a while. Missed me?"

The voice was as smooth as Jack remembered it two decades ago. Ice snaked down his back. He'd forgotten all about the guy years ago. Figured Marcus Wade was dead or in the wind, living in some third-world country.

"What do you want, Marcus?"

The man chuckled. "I see you're still chasing ghosts. Always sticking your nose where it doesn't belong. You haven't changed a bit. You remember where that got us back in the 'Stan? Or, rather, where it got me?"

Jack's grip tightened on the phone. "Yeah, I remember, Marcus. Now, what do you want?"

"I thought I'd give you a little heads-up." Marcus's tone shifted to one of feigned concern. "You're barking up the wrong tree. In fact, you're wrong about a lot of things, old friend."

Jack glanced at Reese, who watched him intently. "You expect me to believe you, *old friend*? After everything you've done?"

"Believe what you want," Marcus said. "But if you're smart, you'll meet with me. We can discuss this face-to-face."

Jack hesitated. He knew better than to trust Marcus. "And why would I do that?"

"Because you want answers. And I'm the only one who can give them to you."

He couldn't shake the feeling that this was a trap. But for who? "I'm not walking into your setup."

Marcus laughed. "Figured you'd say that. Fine, I'll give you something for free. Officer Tilley, the cop you met earlier—he's on Hennessey's payroll. Go talk to him yourself."

"Why should I believe you? What's stopping him from arresting me on the spot?"

"Believe what you want. But you're running out of time." Marcus clicked his tongue. "Tick-tock, Jack."

The line went dead, leaving a heavy silence in its wake. Jack stared at the phone, his mind a whirlwind of suspicion and anger. The familiar voice of Marcus Wade had stirred up a storm of emotions he had tried to bury for years. The bitterness of betrayal, the sting of regret, and the smoldering fury of unresolved vengeance all surged to the surface. Doubt gnawed at him—was this another one of Marcus's twisted games, or was there truth in his taunts? Jack's jaw tightened, his grip on the phone turning his knuckles white. The uncertainty was maddening, but one thing was clear: They couldn't afford to ignore this lead. With a deep breath, he pushed the thoughts aside and focused on the task at hand. They had to find Officer Tilley and uncover the truth, no matter where it led.

"What did he say?" Reese's brow furrowed with concern.

"He claims Officer Tilley is working for Hennessey. And he wants to meet. But I don't trust him."

"Do you think he's telling the truth about Tilley?"

"I don't know," Jack said. "But we can't ignore it. Tilley was on my ass my first day in town. We need to find him and see what he knows. Why don't we start by digging into Tilley's financials."

Reese opened her laptop. "On it. If Marcus is right, there'll be a trail." Her fingers flew across the keyboard as she accessed public records and databases. She cross-referenced Tilley's bank statements, looking for any irregularities. "Got something," Reese said after a few minutes. "There are several large deposits into his account over the past year. All from a company that's a known front for Hennessey's operations."

Jack leaned over her shoulder. "That's our connection. He's on Hennessey's payroll. Guess that's one point for Marcus."

"We need to confront him," Reese said.

Jack nodded. "We need a plan. Let's gather all the evidence we have and approach him when he's alone, off duty. We can't risk him alerting Hennessey."

"I've seen him at Lacy's plenty. We can start there."

As they entered the bar, Jack spotted Tilley sitting at a table at the back, nursing a pint of beer. When he noticed Jack, the man looked surprised. He shifted in his seat, as though he were about to bolt.

"Officer Tilley." Jack sat opposite him. "We need to talk."

Reese sat beside Jack. "We know about the payments you've been receiving from Hennessey."

Tilley's cheeks darkened. "Don't know what the hell you're on about."

Jack leaned forward. "Don't lie to us. We have the evidence. Suspicious deposits, ties to shell companies. You're on Hennessey's payroll."

Tilley glanced around the bar. "Keep your voice down. I don't know what you *think* you have, but it's not what it looks like."

Reese placed a folder on the table. "We have bank records, financial transactions. You're deep in this, Tilley. Come clean to us, or to your superiors. It's your choice."

Tilley's hands trembled as he looked at the evidence. The seconds stretched into a minute. "Look, I didn't have a choice. They threatened me, my family. I had to do what they said."

"What did they want you to do?" Jack said.

Tilley swallowed hard, his eyes darting between Jack and Reese. "Turn a blind eye. Ignore certain activities. Make reports disappear. I didn't know the full extent of what was happening, I swear."

Reese's gaze was unyielding. "You expect us to believe that?"

Tilley's shoulders slumped. "Look, I knew it was bad, but I didn't know they'd go as far as murder. I was just trying to protect my family."

"Not buying it," Jack said.

"What do I need to do to convince you?"

"If you wanna make this right, you need to help us. We need information on Hennessey's operations."

Tilley hesitated, fear on into his face. "If I help you, they'll kill me."

"If you don't help us, more people will die." Reese leaned back. "Brenda's already dead because of this. You need to do the right thing."

Tilley took a deep breath, then nodded slowly. "There's a facility. Hennessey's major event—it's being coordinated there. It's hidden, off the grid. I can give you the location."

Jack nodded. "That's a start. Give us everything you have. We'll do what we can to protect you."

Tilley scribbled down the address of the facility, his hand shaking.

Jack took the paper. "You should get out of town for a bit. Let us handle this."

Tilley drained his beer, looked up at Jack. "Good luck. You'll need it."

Jack and Reese drove back to the cabin. When they arrived, Ben was waiting on the porch. He paced one end to the other.

"What did you find out?" Ben asked as they stepped out of the Jeep.

Jack handed him the paper with the facility's location. "Tilley gave us this. Says it's a hidden facility where Hennessey's planning his next move."

Ben scanned the paper. "This could be the break we've been looking for. But it's going to be dangerous. Hennessey won't leave it unguarded."

Reese pulled out the documents they had gathered earlier. "We need to figure out what we're dealing with."

They spread out the papers on the table. The facility was located in a remote area, well away from prying eyes. It wasn't marked on any of the maps they had seen. Wasn't mentioned in any of the communications they'd found. They assumed it was heavily fortified, with multiple security measures in place.

"This isn't going to be easy," Jack said, tracing the perimeter of the facility on a map. "We'll need to be strategic about our approach. We can't just barge in this time."

Reese studied the map. "We'll need to disable the security systems first. If we can get in undetected, we might be able to gather the evidence we need without alerting Hennessey's men."

Ben looked up from the documents. "There's mention of a control room here. If we can access it, we could shut down the security systems and create a window for us to move in."

Jack formulated a plan in his mind. "We'll need to split up. Ben, you'll stay here with Mark and monitor the situation remotely. Reese and I will infiltrate the facility, disable the security, and gather as much evidence as we can."

Ben's eyes were filled with worry. "Be careful, both of you. This is our best shot, but it's also our riskiest move yet."

Once the details were ironed out, Jack and Reese took a moment to gather their thoughts.

Jack looked at Reese. "No matter what happens, I want you to know that I trust you with my life."

Reese met his gaze. "And I trust you with mine."

CHAPTER 19

Jack and Reese were on the road again. They hadn't made it five minutes when Jack's phone buzzed, the screen lighting up with an unknown number. His gut tightened as he answered, knowing exactly who it would be.

"Hello again, old friend. Did you enjoy your little chat with Tilley?" Marcus's voice dripped with smug satisfaction.

Jack's grip on the phone tightened. "What do you want now, Marcus?"

Reese glanced over.

"I just wanted to remind you that I was right about Tilley. You see, I've always been one step ahead. And you're still playing catch-up. It's almost sad."

"Cut to the chase."

"Ah, straight to business. Very well. I thought I'd give you a heads-up about that facility you're so eager to infiltrate. It's a death trap. Hennessey has it locked down tight. You walk in there, you're not walking out."

"And why should I believe you? Why would you want to help me?"

Marcus chuckled. "Because I have no reason to lie to you.

You're chasing shadows. If you want to take down Hennessey, you need a smarter plan. Meet with me, and I'll show you a safer way."

Jack hesitated. The last thing he wanted was to trust Marcus, but they couldn't afford to walk into a trap. "Last time I saw you, you tried to kill me."

"Let's just say I have my own reasons for wanting Hennessey out of the picture. Think about it, pal. Your move."

Jack said nothing.

"One more thing before I go."

"What?"

"Your buddy Ben isn't exactly who you think he is. Might want to do a little research."

The line went dead.

Jack lowered the phone slowly, tension etched in every line of his face. Marcus's taunting words had stirred a hornet's nest of emotions. The man had a talent for getting under his skin, for making him doubt everything and everyone.

Jack turned to Reese, who watched him intently. "Marcus says the facility is a death trap. He wants us to meet with him."

Reese bit her bottom lip. "And you believe him?"

"I don't know what to believe. But he's been right so far. He also said something else, something that's been gnawing at me. He sowed doubt about Ben's loyalty."

"Ben? But he's been with us this whole time. What proof does Marcus have?"

Jack shook his head. "I don't know. But we need to be sure. We can't afford any more surprises. We need to investigate further, and maybe talk to Lacy again. She might have noticed something."

"Let's not rush into anything. We need to figure out our next move carefully. If Marcus is playing us, we need to be ready."

Jack agreed. "Let's start by looking into Ben. If there's anything off, we need to know."

Jack and Reese parked a few blocks away from Lacy's bar.

Marcus's accusations clouded the air between them. Ben had been by Jack's side from the beginning. He lured Jack in. Why? He'd figured it was because men like them could sense something about the other. Had he been wrong? What if Ben and Marcus were working together? Was it a stretch to think Marcus had warned Jack was coming to town? Only one person knew that, though, and Brandon wasn't going to sell Jack out.

"You okay?" Reese asked.

"Yeah, just mulling all this over," he said.

"Let's think about this rationally. Ben's been with us the whole time. He's helped us every step of the way. But if there's any truth to what Marcus said, we need to find it. Due diligence. Right?"

Jack nodded. "We need to look through his belongings, his communications. Anything that might give us a clue."

"Let's see what Lacy has to say."

They entered the bar. The smell of bison burgers and beer hit them. The usual crowd of locals mingled in the dim light. Lacy looked up from behind the bar as they walked in, concern on her face.

"Back so soon? What's going on?" she asked.

Jack and Reese took seats at the bar.

"We need to ask you about Ben," Jack said.

Lacy's eyes narrowed. "What about him?"

"Have you noticed anything strange about his behavior lately?" Reese asked. "Anything that might suggest he's hiding something?"

Lacy frowned as she wiped her hands on a towel. "He's been coming in more often, that's for sure. Always seems on edge. I thought it was just the stress of everything going on."

Jack eased in. "Has he mentioned meeting anyone, or have you seen him talking to anyone suspicious?"

Lacy thought for a moment. "There was one guy. Looked shady. Then again, everyone looks shady to me these days." She chuckled. "He met Ben a few times in the back. I didn't think much of it at the time, but now...."

"Did you catch any details about this guy?" Reese asked. "Anything at all?"

Lacy shook her head. "Not really. I can't remember every face that comes in here. Just had a bad vibe about him. Sorry I can't be more help."

As they left the bar, Jack and Reese exchanged worried glances. The pieces were starting to come together, but the picture wasn't clear yet.

"We need to confront Ben," Jack said. "We can't go on like this, not knowing if we can trust him."

They returned to the cabin, but found it empty. Ben and Mark were gone. Jack's heart raced as they searched the cabin, finally finding Ben's laptop still open on the table. The screen displayed an email sent to an unknown recipient, discussing a meeting location. It was vague but raised enough suspicion.

"Reese, you need to see this," Jack called.

Reese joined him. She read the email quickly. "This doesn't prove anything, but it's definitely strange. Why wouldn't he tell us about this?"

Jack's phone buzzed, breaking the silence. It was Officer Tilley. Jack answered. "Tilley, what's going on?"

Tilley's voice was urgent. "Ben and Mark were in an accident. They've been taken to the hospital. It doesn't look good for Mark."

Jack's stomach dropped. "We're on our way." He hung up and turned to Reese. "We need to get to the hospital. Now."

When they arrived, they were directed to the emergency room where Tilley was waiting. The room was a flurry of activity, with nurses and doctors moving swiftly between patients, the beeping of monitors and the murmur of medical staff creating a constant background noise. The fluorescent lights cast a harsh glow, illuminating the sterile, white-tiled walls. Tilley stood near the entrance, his face pale and drawn, contrasting starkly with the vibrant scrubs of the hospital staff bustling around him. The air was thick with the scent of antiseptic, mingling with the faint, metallic tang of blood.

"What happened?" Jack said.

Tilley ran a hand through his hair. "It looks like they were run off the road. Ben's stable, but Mark ... he's in critical condition."

"Where's Ben?" Reese asked.

"Room 204. He's been asking for you."

Jack and Reese hurried to Ben's room. They found him lying in bed, bruised and battered but conscious. He looked up as they entered, guilt and pain on his face.

"What happened?" Jack asked.

Ben winced as he tried to sit up. "We were on our way back when a car came out of nowhere. Forced us off the road. I think it was Hennessey's men. They must have found out I was getting too close."

"Why didn't you tell us about the email, Ben?" Reese asked, her voice a mix of concern and frustration. "Why keep us in the dark?"

"What email?"

"The one on your laptop, arranging a meeting."

Ben sighed and winced. He grabbed his side. Probably had a couple busted ribs. "I thought I was protecting you. The less you knew, the safer you were. I was trying to get closer to Hennessey's men, to gather more intel. I didn't think they'd come after me like this."

"That's where you were headed?" Reese asked. "To meet with him?"

Ben didn't reply.

Jack studied Ben's face, searching for any sign of deception. "Marcus warned us about you. Said you weren't who we thought you were."

Ben wouldn't look at Jack.

"He said you couldn't be trusted."

Ben shook his head. "I'm on your side. I've been trying to take Hennessey down from the inside. I never meant for any of this to happen." He leaned back and closed his eyes. "I'll tell you everything. But first, we need to make sure Mark is safe. If Hennessey's men are willing to go this far, they won't stop until we're all out of the picture."

Jack and Reese decided to leave Ben to rest and heal. They needed more information, and Lacy seemed like the best bet. They returned to the bar, where Lacy greeted them with a worried look.

"You two again. What happened? You look like you've seen a ghost."

Jack sat down at the bar. "We need your help again, Lacy. Ben and Mark were in an accident. We think Hennessey's men are behind it."

"Oh my God. Is Ben okay?"

"Ben's stable, but Mark's in critical condition," Reese said. "We need to know if you've seen or heard anything else that might help us."

Lacy leaned over the bar, her voice low. "There's been a lot of talk around town. People are scared. Hennessey's got his fingers in everything. If Ben's been poking around, it's no surprise they came after him."

"Do you know where we can find more information about Hennessey's operations?" Jack asked. "Anything that might help us take him down?"

Lacy thought for a moment. "There's a guy who comes in here sometimes. Works for Hennessey, but he's not happy about it. Name's Joe. He might know something. I can try to set up a meeting."

Jack tapped the bar top. "Do it. Set it up. We need all the help we can get at this point."

They stayed for a drink. The bar atmosphere washed away some of the pain and stress of everything they'd been through. After a short while, Jack and Reese settled into comfortable conversation, like they'd had years ago.

"What's next for you?" she asked him.

Jack shrugged. "Not sure. I knew I had to get here, tell you about your brother. Hadn't thought much beyond that. I want to get back to Mia at some point, but that feels selfish."

"Why?" Reese placed her hand on his.

"I'm not really much of a dad. I know Sean is doing a better job raising her than I ever could. And she's got her cousins, who are more like siblings at this point."

"You miss her?"

"Of course." Jack lifted his bourbon and took a sip. "Doesn't mean I need to uproot her, mess up her life. Every day with me is a year in therapy twenty years from now. Is it really responsible to do that to her?"

Reese sighed. "Wish I had one of my own."

Jack offered a smile. "There's still time."

"Gotta find the right guy though." She squeezed his hand. "Thought I had him, but he kept slipping away."

He stared in her eyes for a few moments. The perfect place to get lost. Reese was a mirage of everything he ever wanted. She had little connection to his past. She offered an uncertain future, but one he could see himself in. But he couldn't offer her the family she wanted.

"Perhaps you should leave him in the past," Jack said.

Reese withdrew her hand. "Perhaps I should." She finished her drink and slid off the barstool. "Let's head back to the hospital and talk to Ben."

CHAPTER 20

BACK AT THE HOSPITAL, JACK AND REESE SAT DOWN WITH Ben, ready to hear his full story.

"Start from the beginning," Jack said. "Tell us everything."

Ben took a deep breath. "I've been working undercover, trying to infiltrate Hennessey's organization. I knew it was dangerous, but I didn't realize how deep it went. When I started getting close, they must have found out. That's when the threats started."

"You were working with Brenda the whole time?" Jack asked.

Ben closed his eyes and turned his head to the side. A single tear slid down his cheek. "I got her involved in this mess. If it weren't for me—"

"She'd be alive." Jack wrapped his hands around the back of his head. "Who else have you pulled into this? Aside from me and Reese."

"I can't trust anyone here," Ben said. "Hennessey has his hands in everything. But you, you're an outsider. I could tell right away that you were a man who could get things done."

"And the email?" Reese asked.

Ben nodded. "It was a contact. Someone inside Hennessey's

operation who was willing to talk. I didn't tell you because I didn't want to jeopardize what we're doing here."

Jack's anger simmered just below the surface. "You should have trusted us. Hell, you didn't even know me and brought me into this mess."

"I know," Ben said, his voice breaking. "I'm sorry. I was trying to protect you."

"We have a lead on a guy named Joe," Jack said. "Lacy's going to set up a meeting so we can see if he knows anything."

"I know him," Ben said. "Can't say you'll get too much info out of him. At least, I couldn't."

"What do you know about him?" Jack asked.

Ben rubbed his temples. "Joe's a ghost. He hasn't been in town for long—maybe a couple of months. Nobody knows much about his past or what he does for a living. He keeps a low profile, which is probably why Hennessey likes him."

"What's his role in Hennessey's organization?" Reese asked.

"From what I gathered, Joe's a fixer. He handles problems, makes things disappear. People, evidence, whatever Hennessey needs. I've seen him a few times, always on the periphery, never getting his hands dirty directly."

Jack frowned. "And you couldn't get any more out of him?"

Ben shook his head. "He's cautious, paranoid even. Keeps his cards close to his chest. I tried to approach him, but he brushed me off. He's not the type to trust easily, especially not strangers."

"But if he's that careful, why is he meeting with Lacy?" Reese asked.

"Lacy's got a way with people. She's connected, and she knows how to make people talk. Maybe Joe sees her as a neutral party, someone who can be trusted to some extent."

Jack took it all in. "We need to handle this carefully. If Joe senses a trap, he'll disappear, and we'll lose a valuable lead."

Reese agreed. "We'll need to play it cool, make him feel like he's in control. Let's hope Lacy can work her magic."

Jack and Reese sat in tense silence, the hum of hospital machinery and distant chatter filling the room as they absorbed Ben's words.

"Why didn't you tell us everything from the start?" Jack asked. "Did you already know about the things we uncovered at the safe house, the warehouse?"

Ben hesitated. "I had my suspicions. I knew Brenda was onto something big, but I didn't have all the pieces. I needed you to confirm what I suspected, to find the evidence I couldn't."

Reese's eyes narrowed. "You used us."

Ben shook his head. "No, it wasn't like that. I needed help, and I couldn't trust anyone else. Hennessey has eyes everywhere. You two were my best chance at bringing him down."

"And what about now, Ben?" Jack said. "Is there anything else you're not telling us? Anything that could help us, or that could get us killed?"

Ben took a deep breath. "There is something. Something I haven't told anyone. But you need to understand, I was trying to protect you, to keep you safe."

"What is it?" Reese asked.

Ben opened his mouth to speak, but hesitated, his eyes flicking to the door. Just as he was about to reveal his secret, the overhead speakers crackled to life.

"Code blue, room 214. Code blue, room 214."

Jack's heart sank. The blood drained from his face as the gravity of the situation hit him. He glanced at Reese, her eyes mirroring his concern and fear. Without a word, he bolted out of the room, his pulse quickening with every step.

The hospital corridor buzzed with urgency, a flurry of medical staff in scrubs and white coats rushing toward Mark's room. The wheels of a gurney squeaked against the polished floor, and the overhead lights flickered slightly as if responding to the sudden rush of energy. Nurses and doctors moved with practiced efficiency, their faces masks of intense concentration.

Jack weaved through the sea of hospital personnel, his eyes fixed on the door to Mark's room. Reese was right behind him, her breath coming in short, sharp bursts. The air was thick with the antiseptic smell of the hospital. As they neared the room, the sound of urgent, muffled voices and the steady beep of medical equipment filled their ears. The scene inside was chaotic, a stark contrast to the sterile, controlled environment outside.

Jack noticed a man standing at the end of the hallway. The dim lighting cast eerie patterns across his features. Jack couldn't make out his face. The man's posture was relaxed, too casual for the chaos unfolding in the hall.

As their eyes met, a shiver ran down Jack's spine. The man's lips curled into a smile, a gesture that felt both taunting and sinister. Jack's instincts screamed that this was no coincidence. Before he could react, the man turned on his heel and disappeared around the corner with an unsettling calmness, as if he had all the time in the world.

Jack surged forward. Adrenaline pumped through his veins. He sprinted down the hallway, his footsteps echoing off the sterile walls. But by the time he reached the corner, the man was gone.

He cursed under his breath and rushed back to Mark's room. His footsteps pounded against the floor, each step echoing his rising panic. As he approached the doorway, the scene before him made his heart sink. The small room was a flurry of activity. Doctors and nurses crowded around the bed.

Monitors beeped frantically. Their erratic sounds were a stark contrast to the tense silence of the hallway. Tubes and wires snaked around Mark's motionless body, and the medical team worked tirelessly, their movements a blur as they administered chest compressions and prepared defibrillator paddles.

Mark's face was ashen and still. The sight confirmed his worst fears. The doctors' frantic efforts seemed futile, a desperate attempt to reclaim a life that was slipping away. Jack felt a lump form in his throat, a mix of anger, frustration, and helplessness washing over him. The reality of the situation hit him hard—Mark was dying, and there was nothing he could do to stop it. And any information Mark had would die with him.

A nurse exited the room and approached them. "Excuse me, you two need to step back," she said firmly. "We're doing everything we can in there." She didn't wait for either to reply. She turned her back on them and let the door to Mark's room fall shut.

Jack looked at Reese and held his hands in front of him, frustrated. "Let's wait with Ben."

He and Reese returned to Ben's room, but it was empty. Panic surged through Jack as he scanned the room, then the hallway again. Ben was gone. Had he snuck out amid the confusion in the hallway? Had the guy at the end of the hall had something to do with it? Was that man working with a partner?

"Where the hell is he?" Reese said.

Jack's gaze darted around the room, searching for any clue. "I don't know. But he couldn't have gone far."

A nurse passing by did a double take. She entered the room. "What are you two doing in here?"

"Our friend," Jack said. "Where is he?"

The nurse frowned, puzzled. "I'm not sure. He shouldn't have left. We're in the middle of an emergency right now. You two wait here."

"Ben wouldn't just leave," Reese said. "He was too injured to go far on his own."

"We need to find him. He might be in danger." They stepped out into the hallway. "Let's check the desk in the waiting room."

There was no sign of Ben, and the lady at the desk said she hadn't seen anything. Jack felt a growing sense of dread. Just moments ago, they had been on the brink of getting crucial information from Ben. Now, not only was Mark dead, but Ben had vanished without a trace. Jack couldn't shake the feeling that they were being watched, that whoever had been at the end of the hallway had something to do with this.

"Let's check the exits," Jack said, his tone resolute. "He couldn't have gotten far on his own."

As they hurried down the hallway, Jack couldn't help but feel that time was running out. The stakes had never been higher, and the margin for error had never been thinner.

"Where could he have gone?" Reese asked, her voice tinged with worry.

Jack's mind raced. "He must have known we'd come back for answers. Maybe he's on the run, but we need to find him before Hennessey does."

Reese jutted her chin to a door. "Security. Maybe they have footage."

Jack didn't bother knocking. He barreled right into the room. The security guard on duty was startled, but before he could say anything, Jack said, "We need to review the last fifteen minutes of footage."

The man rose, waving both hands in front of him. "The hell you think you are barging in here like this?"

"Stop wasting time. We need to review the footage."

"Good luck," the guard said. "System's been down for half an hour. Waiting on our IT guy to show up now."

Frustrated, Jack threw his hands in the air and kicked the door into the wall on his way out of the room. The man behind the desk was on his radio, calling for backup. By the time they reached the waiting room, two additional guards stood waiting.

"That's them," the first guard called from behind them.

"Don't bother," Jack said. "We were just leaving."

CHAPTER 21

JACK AND REESE SPED AWAY FROM THE HOSPITAL. THE frustration of losing Ben gnawed at them, but they couldn't afford to waste any time. They began circling the hospital, searching every corner, alley, and parking lot in the immediate area for any sign of Ben.

"Keep your eyes peeled," Jack said. "He couldn't have gotten far on foot."

"If he's on foot," Reese said.

They drove slowly, scrutinizing every pedestrian, every parked car, hoping for a glimpse of their missing ally. The minutes ticked by, but there was no sign of Ben.

"We're not going to find him like this," Reese said. "We need to think about where he might go. If he's trying to stay hidden, he wouldn't just wander around aimlessly."

"The cabin. We need to go back to the cabin. He might have headed there, thinking it's a safe place."

"But what if it's not safe?" Reese said. "What if someone's there, waiting for us?"

Jack had already considered this. The risks were great. "We

need the evidence we have there. We can't just leave it. And if Ben is there, we need to get him out."

The drive to the cabin was tense, each of them lost in their thoughts. Jack tried not to let his mind race with the possibilities. There'd be time for that. Right now, he had to remain focused and ready for anything at the cabin.

As they rounded the final bend, the cabin came into view, and Jack's heart dropped. Flames licked the night sky, their vibrant orange and red tongues dancing against the darkness. The structure was engulfed in a roaring inferno, the heat palpable even from a distance. Thick, black smoke billowed upward in ominous, swirling columns, obscuring the stars and creating a suffocating haze. The crackling of burning wood filled the air, interspersed with the occasional pop and hiss as the fire consumed everything in its path. The once sturdy walls of the cabin were now a crumbling, charred skeleton. The roof collapsed inward with a thunderous crash. The acrid smell of burning timber and ash stung their nostrils.

Reese covered her mouth, her eyes wide with horror. "We're too late. Everything ... all the evidence...."

Jack tried to process the scene. The cabin was a total loss, the fire too intense for them to even consider approaching. "We need to see if there's anything we can salvage," he said, though he knew it was a longshot.

They circled the perimeter, keeping a safe distance from the flames. Jack's heart sank further as he realized the extent of the destruction. Whoever had set this fire had made sure there would be nothing left.

Reese's voice broke through his thoughts. "Jack, look."

She pointed to a trail leading away from the cabin. It was faint, but unmistakable—footprints in the dirt, heading toward the woods.

"Ben?" Jack said.

"Could be," Reese said. "But it could also be whoever did this."

Jack nodded. "Let's go. Stay alert."

They moved quickly but cautiously, following the trail into the woods. The sounds of the burning cabin faded as they delved deeper into the trees, replaced by the rustle of leaves.

Every step felt like a gamble, the shadows around them playing tricks on their eyes. Jack's senses were on high alert. Every snap of a twig sent a jolt of adrenaline through his system. They followed the footprints, hoping they were on the right track, knowing that every second counted.

"Jack," Reese whispered, pointing ahead.

In the dim light, they saw a figure lying on the ground. Jack's heart pounded as they approached.

As they drew closer, the figure stirred, revealing a familiar face. It was Ron, Lacy's ex-husband and one half of the father-and-son Leak Geeks team. He was injured and struggling to move. His face was bruised and swollen, with a deep gash above his right eyebrow. One arm hung at an awkward angle, and his clothes were torn and bloodstained. His breathing was labored, each inhale accompanied by a wince of pain.

"Ron!" Jack and Reese rushed to his side.

Ron looked up, pain on his face. He licked his lips before speaking. "They—they were waiting for me. I had to run. They set the place on fire."

"What were you doing here?" Jack said.

"Ben asked me to meet him here."

"Why?"

"I'm not sure."

"We need to get him out of here," Reese said.

"Can you walk?" Jack said.

Ron nodded weakly. "I think so. But we need to hurry. They might come back."

Jack and Reese helped Ron to his feet, supporting him as they made their way back to the car. The fire raged behind them, a stark reminder of the dangers they faced. The acrid smoke burned their lungs and eyes, but they pressed on, determined to get Ron to safety.

As they reached the Jeep, Jack looked back at the burning cabin. "We need to find out what happened here. And where Ben is."

Reese nodded. "But first, let's get Ron to a safe place and get him some help."

"We can't go back to the hospital."

"Let's bring him to Lacy's then."

THEY DROVE TO LACY'S BAR. THE STREETS WERE NEARLY empty, bathed in the dim glow of streetlights. The bar's neon sign flickered in the darkness, casting light intermittently on the aged pavement. Jack parked the Jeep, and they helped Ron out, supporting his weight between them. His every step was labored. Each movement elicited a wince of pain.

Lacy was just about to close up when they came in. The interior of the bar was quiet, with only a few stragglers finishing their drinks. She looked up from wiping down the counter, her eyes widening in shock at the sight of them. The sight of Ron's bloodied and bruised form made her gasp, and she dropped the cloth she was holding.

"What happened?" she asked, rushing over to help. Her voice was filled with concern and panic as she took in Ron's injuries—his bruised face, the gash on his forehead, his broken arm hanging at an awkward angle.

The patrons at the bar glanced over curiously, but a stern look from Jack kept them from asking questions.

"Can we take him in back? Jack said. "It's not safe to take him to a hospital right now."

Lacy hurried to the door and waved them forward. "Of course. Bring him through." She led them past the bar and through a narrow hallway to a small, private room at the back. The room was lit with fluorescent lighting. A few old chairs and a table cluttered with papers and empty glasses adorned the area. The faint smell of stale beer hung in the air.

Lacy grabbed a first aid kit from a cabinet and tended to Ron's wounds with practiced hands. She dabbed antiseptic on the gash on his forehead, and he flinched, sucking in a sharp breath.

"What happened to you, Ron?" Lacy asked, her voice trembling as she worked. She glanced up at Jack and Reese, her expression a mix of fear and confusion.

Ron winced again as she cleaned his wound. "Ben asked me to meet him at the cabin. Said he had something important to discuss. But when I got there, the place was already on fire. I tried to get out, but they caught me."

"Who caught you?" Jack pressed, leaning in closer. His eyes were intense, searching Ron's face for any clue. "Where was your car?"

Ron shook his head. "I don't know. I don't know. They wore masks. Said something about making sure we didn't find out the truth. And I guess they took my car."

Reese exchanged a worried glance with Jack. "We need to find Ben. He could be in serious danger."

"What happened to Ben?" Lacy asked.

Jack filled her in on what had happened at the hospital.

"Mark may've had it coming. Ben, too, I suppose. He's been digging for a while. With good reason, I'll add. But digging is digging, and sometimes you strike a sewer line and end up covered in shit." Lacy finished bandaging Ron's wounds. She splinted his arm. "I'll take care of him. You two go find Ben. And be careful."

"We'll want to talk with you tomorrow, Ron," Jack said.

Ron nodded. "I won't go anywhere."

"Come on, Reese. Let's get moving."

CHAPTER 22

JACK AND REESE STOOD JUST OUTSIDE LACY'S BAR. THE NIGHT air was cool. The clouds began to obscure the night sky, casting the street in a somber shadow. The occasional distant rumble of thunder hinted at an approaching storm.

Jack rubbed his temples, trying to think clearly despite the exhaustion weighing him down. His time in town had been nonstop. The intensity of the situation continued to ratchet up. Part of him wanted to bail, just leave it all behind. This wasn't his battle. He found Reese. Delivered the news. He didn't want to abandon her here, but she could go with him. Screw the FBI and witness protection. With him, she'd be safe. He was about to say all that to her when she turned toward him and cleared her throat.

"I'm really worried about Ben. We have to find him."

"We've got nothing to go by."

"Maybe the hospital tech guy restored the footage around the time of his disappearance."

Jack shook his head. "That was a pro job. The system was down for sure. Probably dismantled. We'll never see what happened."

"So what do we do?"

Jack shoved his hands in his pockets and tipped his head back. The sky was completely covered now. "We can't go back to the hospital. Far too dangerous. Guarantee someone is watching it. And honestly, Reese, I need some damn sleep. My gut feeling is we'll be contacted. So, let's rest up and wait for that contact."

"Where should we go?"

"Your place is too risky. If Hennessey's men are looking for us, it'll be one of the first places they check. The Lewiston Inn is our best bet. Sam's place has been secure so far, and we know it's a place we can trust."

Reese glanced back at the bar, her worry evident. "Do you think Ron will be okay with Lacy?"

Jack offered a reassuring nod. "She'll take good care of him. He's safe for now."

With their decision made, they climbed into the Jeep and headed toward the Lewiston Inn. The streets were quiet, the usual hum of activity replaced by an oppressive stillness. As they drove, Jack couldn't help but keep an eye on the rearview mirror, half-expecting to see a tail.

When they arrived at the inn, the familiar sight of the neon vacancy sign flickering in the darkness brought a small measure of comfort. Jack parked the Jeep in the back lot, and they hustled inside the building. The warm glow of the inn's interior was a stark contrast to the tension outside.

They found Sam behind the bar, wiping down glasses and tidying up. He looked up as they entered, a mix of surprise and concern crossing his features. "You two look like you've been through hell. What happened?"

Jack and Reese exchanged a glance before approaching the bar. Jack leaned against the counter, the weight of the night settling heavily on his shoulders. "We lost Ben. The cabin was burned down, and we barely made it out. We need a place to stay for the night and some advice."

Sam's expression darkened as he listened. "Lost? You mean ... he's dead?"

"We don't know," Reese said. "He was hurt in an accident. Him and Mark Cundiff."

Sam nodded. "I know him."

She continued. "Both were in the hospital. Mark was in much worse shape than Ben. Anyway, Mark coded. We went out to see what was happening. Jack saw someone hurrying to leave and went to follow, but lost the guy. The staff lost Mark, and by the time we returned to the room, Ben was gone. Security was no help, had no footage."

"We rushed to Ben's cabin," Jack said.

"I know of it," Sam said.

Reese continued. "It was in flames. The entire thing engulfed. Every shred of evidence we'd found went up in smoke."

"We followed some footprints," Jack said. "Found Ron, Lacy's ex-husband. Beaten up pretty badly. Said he hadn't seen Ben, but was there because Ben asked him to meet him. Not sure who set the fire, but I'd guess it was whoever caused the accident, maybe even the guy I saw in the hospital."

Sam set down his rag and crossed his arms over his chest. "Damn. Sounds like things are getting serious. Let's talk. Maybe I can help."

As they settled onto the barstools, the atmosphere in the inn felt like a fragile sanctuary, a brief respite from the chaos swirling around them. They knew they couldn't stay hidden for long, but for now, it was enough.

The soft murmur of distant conversation and the clinking of glasses created a backdrop that was comforting in its normalcy. Sam's eyes bore into them, filled with a mix of concern and curiosity.

Sam leaned against the counter. "I've been keeping an eye on things around town. Seen some shady stuff going on."

Jack's interest piqued. "Let's get right to it, then. What do you know about Hennessey's operations? We've uncovered bits and pieces, but most of our evidence went up in flames with the cabin. And, honestly, it just felt like a game of Clue. We were going from this place to that, finding sometimes conflicting information, all of it leading to another location that led to another location. It's been frustrating."

Sam nodded. "Sounds about right. Hennessey's a snake. On the surface, he's all about that new development project, making it seem like he's trying to revitalize the town by bringing money in to that spa. But beneath that, there's a whole different story. I've heard whispers, seen some things that don't add up."

Reese leaned in, her eyes locked on Sam. "What kind of things?"

Sam took a deep breath, gathering his thoughts. "The public project, that's just a front. He's talking about new businesses, more jobs, a better future for Lewiston. But the real agenda is far more sinister. He's using that project to cover up a network of illegal activities. Drug trafficking, money laundering, you name it."

Jack exchanged a look with Reese. "We've seen some of the financial records, the shell companies. It all makes sense. But what's his end game?"

Sam rubbed his chin. "Power and control. Hennessey's trying to cement his position as the undisputed ruler of this town. He wants to expand his operations, and Lewiston's just the beginning. He's got contacts in other cities, probably even in law enforcement and politics. Without something solid, you can't just walk up and arrest the guy. Hell, he's got the police locked down here. I wouldn't trust a single one of them."

Reese's lips thinned. "And we're sitting here with nothing to show for our efforts. We need more than just whispers and suspicions."

"I might have something that can help." Sam reached under the counter. He pulled out a worn, leather-bound notebook and slid it across to them. "This belonged to a friend of mine who was looking into Hennessey before he disappeared. It's got names, places, transactions—everything he managed to dig up."

Jack opened the notebook. The pages were filled with meticulous notes and diagrams. "This is gold. With this, we can start piecing things together again."

Sam leaned in closer. "Be careful. Hennessey's men are everywhere, and as you've seen, they're not above using violence to keep their secrets. You need to stay one step ahead."

Jack nodded. "Thanks, Sam. We owe you one."

"Just bring that bastard down," Sam said.

Reese closed the notebook and slipped it into her bag. "We need to get some rest and start fresh in the morning. We've got a lot of work ahead of us."

Jack agreed. "Let's head to my room. We can go over this and plan our next move."

JACK AND REESE THANKED SAM AGAIN BEFORE HEADING upstairs to Jack's room with a bottle of wine. He couldn't shake the exhaustion from the day. The stress. The anxiety. The worry.

Inside the room, Jack locked the door behind them. Reese set the leather-bound notebook on the small table by the window, grabbed two glasses, and dragged a second chair over to the desk. Jack joined her.

He opened the notebook again, skimming through the pages filled with names, addresses, and detailed accounts of Hennessey's dealings. "This is a treasure trove of information. We just need to figure out how to use it."

Reese leaned on his shoulder, reading along with him. "We should start by identifying the key players mentioned here and cross-referencing them with what we already know. We can't afford any mistakes."

They spent the next hour poring over the notebook, cross-referencing names and dates with the fragments of information they still had. It was tedious work, but it felt good to be making progress again. The storm outside finally broke, and rain pattered against the window. The sound was soothing, lulling them into a relaxed state.

"We need to be strategic about our next moves," Jack said. "We can't just go barging into places anymore. We need solid evidence and a plan."

Reese nodded. "Agreed. We also need to consider how we're going to protect ourselves and the people who are helping us. We can't underestimate Hennessey any longer."

"Maybe I should take Marcus Wade up on his offer and meet with him. If I do it someplace public, there's a chance we don't shoot each other."

Reese laughed then apologized for doing so. "Just caught me off guard."

Jack looked at Reese. Really looked at her for the first time since finding her again. She was beautiful. Even after the day they'd had, the woman looked amazing. "You've been incredible through all of this. I know it's been hard, especially with every-thing that's happened to Brenda."

Reese's face softened. "We've both lost people we care about. But that's why we have to see this through. For Brenda, for Ben, for everyone who's been hurt by Hennessey's greed."

They continued to sift through the notebook, finding more connections and potential leads. As the night wore on, their fatigue caught up with them. Jack closed the notebook and leaned back in his chair, running a hand through his hair. Reese leaned against him. Her soft lips brushed his neck. He turned and kissed her.

Jack set the notebook on the nightstand and turned off the light. They settled into the bed, in each other's arms, and let the tension of the day ebb away as the rain continued its steady rhythm against the window.

CHAPTER 23

JACK WOKE TO THE COLD EMPTINESS BESIDE HIM. THE morning light filtered through the curtains, casting a gentle glow across the room. Reese's side of the bed was undisturbed, as if she hadn't been there all night. A knot of unease tightened in his stomach, mingling with the grogginess of sleep. He bolted up, the remnants of sleep vanishing as concern took over. The cool air and the silence of the room heightened his sense of dread, making his heart race faster.

"Reese?" he called out. There was no response.

He swung his legs out of bed and stood. There was no sign of her in the room. That's when he saw it—a note on the nightstand. He hurried over. Her neat handwriting stared back at him. His heart sank as he picked it up and read:

Jack,

I'm leaving town. It's too dangerous here, and I don't want to put you in any more danger. Every time we've tried to be together, circumstances have torn us apart, forcing me into government hiding. I can't live like that anymore. I need to take control of my life and make my own choices, even if it means walking away from everything, including you.

You've done more for me than I can ever repay, and it's tearing me apart to leave you like this. But I need to find a way to live on my own terms, without constantly looking over my shoulder.

Please understand and take this opportunity to leave town, too. You deserve a life free from this chaos.

Love,

Reese

Why had she left so abruptly? What danger was she running from? Hell, he might've gone with her if she had just talked to him instead of disappearing. He crumpled the note in his fist, then flattened it out and folded it. He was going to tuck it into the journal, but that was gone, too.

Jack hurried downstairs, determined to find answers. He found Sam behind the front desk, sorting through some paperwork. The inn was quiet, the calm before the day's activity began.

"Sam," Jack called out as he approached the desk.

Sam looked up, surprise flashing across his face at Jack's urgency. "Morning, Jack. You look like you've seen a ghost."

"Tanya is gone," Jack said. "Did you see her leave?"

Sam shook his head. "No, I didn't. I've been here a little over an hour and no one's been down here. She must've slipped out before that. I'm sorry, Jack. I wish I could tell you more."

Jack rubbed his temples. "She left a note, said she's leaving town because it's too dangerous. Did she say anything to you about her plans?"

"No, she didn't. Not sure why she'd tell me and not you. She seemed a bit on edge last night, but that's about it."

Jack took a deep breath and tried to think clearly. "I need to find her. She might be in serious trouble."

Sam nodded sympathetically. "If you need anything, you know where to find me."

"Thanks, Sam," Jack said, turning to leave. He had to start somewhere, and Reese's house seemed like the logical first step.

Jack drove through the quiet streets of Lewiston. The sun was beginning to rise, casting a pale light over the town. He wished it was would wash over his thoughts. His mind raced with worry and unanswered questions. Reese's note kept replaying in his head, her words a haunting echo that drove him forward.

When he arrived at Reese's house, Jack parked his Jeep a few houses down and approached on foot, staying alert for any signs of danger. The neighborhood was still and silent, the early morning air crisp and cool. The faint glow of the sunrise silhouetted the trees. The occasional chirp of a waking bird the only sound breaking the silence.

As he walked, Jack noticed a tricycle tipped over on a neighbor's lawn, its bright red paint gleaming with morning dew. A newspaper lay abandoned in a driveway, the front-page headline about the town's ongoing construction project. Everything seemed normal, but Jack couldn't shake the feeling he was being watched.

When he reached Reese's house, he took a moment to scan the area. His gaze lingered on a parked sedan with its windows fogged up, an unusual sight for this time of morning. He made a mental note of it as he stepped onto the porch, the creak of the wooden boards under his feet echoing loudly in the stillness.

He let himself in with the key Reese had given him. He called out for her and received no response. He made his way to her bedroom and immediately noticed the disarray. Clothes were strewn across the bed, drawers stood half-open, and a few personal items scattered on the floor. It was clear she had left in a hurry. Jack's heart ached at the thought of her rushing out, scared and alone.

He looked for any clues that might indicate where she had gone. On the dresser, he found a necklace he had given her in Texas, perhaps left behind because she couldn't bear to take it with her. They'd been torn apart twice before. But this time, she made the decision to leave. He picked it up. The cool metal slipped through his fingers. He placed it in his pocket.

As he was about to check the kitchen, Jack heard a noise outside. His muscles tensed with a mix of anxiety and readiness. Footsteps. Damn, who could that be? He listened carefully, every nerve on edge, his mind racing through the possibilities. Had Hennessey's men found him? Was it someone looking for Reese? He moved to the window and peered out. His heart pounding in his chest.

A figure approached the house. His breath caught as he recognized the familiar silhouette. Tilley. What the hell was he doing here? This couldn't be a coincidence. Tilley was on Hennessey's payroll, wasn't he? So what did he want now? Arrest Jack? Take him out? Either way, Jack couldn't let Tilley get the jump on him.

Jack cursed under his breath. He had to get out, but it was too late. Tilley was already at the door. Jack backed away.

The door swung open, and Tilley stepped inside, gun drawn.

"Jack Noble," he said. "You're under arrest."

Jack raised his hands slightly. "On what charges?"

"Obstruction of justice, resisting arrest, and suspicion of involvement in recent criminal activities." Tilley pulled out a pair of handcuffs. "Turn around and put your hands behind your back."

Jack knew he couldn't let himself be taken in, not now. He had to find Reese and figure out what was really going on. "Tilley, listen to me. You don't understand what's happening here."

"I understand perfectly," Tilley said, stepping closer. "Now, turn around."

Jack pretended to comply. Once he saw Tilley let his guard down slightly, Jack lunged forward. He caught Tilley off guard. The confined space of the room made it difficult to move. Jack managed to knock the pistol out of Tilley's hand, sending it skittering across the floor. He punched Tilley in the gut, then shoved him. The officer stumbled backward over a chair.

Jack grabbed the handcuffs, attached one end around Tilley's wrist, and the other to the radiator pipe. Then he bolted out the door and sprinted down the street to his Jeep. He heard Tilley shouting after him but didn't look back. He needed to get away. Needed to regroup and figure out his next move.

The most logical place he could think to go was Lacy's. He hurried over and pulled into a spot out front. The place was just opening. They served breakfast Friday through Sunday. He pulled the door open and saw half the tables seated. The normal smell of bison burger had been replaced with bacon.

Lacy looked as though she had barely slept, which made sense if she took care of Ron all night.

"Jack, what's going on?" she asked.

"Reese is gone," Jack said.

"Who?"

Jack bit down, having forgotten only a few people knew her real identity. "Tanya. She left a note saying she's leaving town, and encouraged me to do the same. But I think she's in danger. And Tilley just tried to arrest me at her place. I need to know if you've seen her or if you know anything that can help."

"I haven't seen her since you two left last night. She hasn't said anything about leaving. But if Tilley's after you, this is serious."

Jack nodded. "I need to stay ahead of him and figure out where Reese is. Anything you can tell me might help."

Lacy glanced around. All eyes were on them. "Come to the back. We can talk there."

Jack followed her to a small back room. The noise of the bar faded as they closed the door behind them. Lacy turned to face him. "Jack, I've heard some things about Hennessey's plans. I had no idea Ron was in so deep. If Reese is caught up in this, you're both in more danger than you realize."

"Tell me everything," Jack said.

As Lacy spoke, Jack felt a flicker of hope. She was usually so guarded, but now she was opening up completely.

"Jack, there's something you need to know about Hennessey's plans," she began. "He's been using the development project as a cover for his real operations. The spa is just a front. Hennessey's been laundering money through a network of shell companies tied to the construction and related businesses."

"I'm aware of the shell companies. What kind of businesses, though?"

"Everything from fake consulting firms to bogus supply companies. He's funneling money through these entities to make it look legitimate, but it's all dirty money from drug trafficking and illegal arms deals," Lacy explained. "He's been expanding his influence, not just in Lewiston, but across the state. He's got people in his pocket in law enforcement, local government, even the state legislature."

"Ron told you all of this last night?"

Lacy glanced down at her desk. "I may be more aware than I've let on. Shit, Jack, all of us are."

This was bigger than he had imagined. "Why hasn't anyone stopped him?"

"Because he's smart," Lacy said. "He keeps his hands clean, uses intermediaries to do his dirty work. And he's ruthless. Anyone who gets too close, like Brenda, ends up dead or missing."

"Like Ben, too."

"And almost Ron." She shook her head. "Honestly, it would've been a favor to me." She smiled at her own joke, but it faded quickly.

"Going after him directly isn't the right play. With no one on my side, it's too risky. I'll get slaughtered. We need to expose him. Get enough evidence to bring him down."

Lacy nodded. "There's more. Hennessey's planning something

big. He's been bringing in shipments through the old warehouse district. Rumor has it he's got a major deal going down soon, something that could solidify his power. If we can find out what it is, maybe we can stop it and gather the proof we need."

"I need to find out when and where this deal is happening. If we can catch him in the act, we can take him down for good."

Lacy hesitated. "There's one more thing. I heard he's got someone on the inside, feeding him information. That's why he's always a step ahead. We need to find out who the mole is and cut off his advantage."

"Apparently, that could be anybody."

They both turned at the sound of someone yelling from the bar.

"The hell?" Jack reached for the door, but it whipped open before he grabbed the handle. His heart sank as he saw Tilley standing there, two officers flanking him.

"Jack Noble, you're under arrest," Tilley said. "And this time, you're not getting away."

CHAPTER 24

Jᴀᴄᴋ'ꜱ ʜᴀɴᴅꜱ ᴡᴇʀᴇ ᴄᴜꜰꜰᴇᴅ ᴛɪɢʜᴛʟʏ ʙᴇʜɪɴᴅ ʜɪꜱ ʙᴀᴄᴋ ᴀꜱ Tilley and the officers led him to the squad car. He didn't resist. Struggling would only make things worse. The ride to the station was a blur. His mind raced with thoughts of Reese, Hennessey, and the ever-tightening noose around his neck. When they arrived, the routine of booking began. Jack felt a sense of detachment as he was processed, almost as if he were watching from outside his own body.

The officer at the desk barked commands. "Name?"

Jack didn't respond.

Tilley said, "Jack Noble."

"Occupation?"

Jack ignored the question.

Tilley said, "Private Investigator."

They took his fingerprints. The ink felt cold and sticky on his fingers. The mug shots came next, the bright flash of the camera blinding him momentarily. The officer then gathered his personal effects, including his wallet, phone, and the necklace he had taken from Reese's house.

"You'll get these back when you're released," the officer said in a practiced tone that told Jack he'd rather be anywhere else than the station that day.

Jack felt hollow. An emptiness pervaded his soul, a void that seemed to consume him from the inside out as they led him down the hallway to the holding cells. The sterile, fluorescent lights cast a harsh glare on the cold, concrete walls, and the echo of his footsteps sounded distant and detached. Each step felt heavy, as if he were trudging through thick mud. He barely noticed the officers beside him, their voices a distant murmur as his thoughts spiraled into the dark recesses of his mind.

The cell door clanged shut behind him. The sound reverberated off the concrete walls. Jack sat on the hard bench and the cold seeped through his clothes. The cell was small, barely big enough for the bench and a metal toilet in the corner. A single overhead light buzzed faintly, casting harsh shadows across the room.

Jack leaned back against the wall, closing his eyes. His thoughts once again drifted to Reese. Where was she? Was she safe? He replayed the events of the past few days in his mind, trying to piece together any clues he might have missed. Was there anything she said that could hint at where she went? The worry gnawed at him, but he forced himself to stay calm. Panic never helped.

The cell door creaked open, and a man stumbled in, reeking of alcohol. He was middle-aged, with unkempt hair and clothes that looked like they hadn't been washed in weeks. The man slumped onto the bench opposite Jack, muttering to himself.

"Great, just what I need," Jack thought, shifting slightly to give the man some space.

The drunk mumbled incoherently, his words slurred and barely audible. Jack tried to ignore him, focusing on his own thoughts. But as the minutes ticked by, he couldn't help but listen to the man's ramblings.

"...Hennessey...bastard...ruined everything..."

Jack's ears perked up at the mention of Hennessey. He turned his attention to the drunk, who continued to mutter, oblivious to Jack's scrutiny.

"... saw them ... warehouse ... something big..."

Jack leaned forward. "What did you say about Hennessey?"

The drunk blinked, his bleary eyes struggling to focus on Jack. "Hennessey? That bastard. Got his fingers in everything, he does. Heard them talking 'bout some big deal ... warehouse district ..."

Could this drunk actually have useful information?

"When did you hear this? What deal?"

The man rubbed his face and searched the ceiling for his memories. "Couple days ago, maybe. Was at the bar ... Hennessey's men were talking, didn't think I was listening. Said something 'bout a shipment, big money. Couldn't make out much more."

Jack steadied himself, not wanting to show his excitement. This was more than he had expected. "Do you remember which bar?"

"Yeah, yeah ... Lacy's place. They like to hang out there, think it's safe. But I hear things, you know?"

"What kind of things do you hear?"

The drunk swayed a bit, his eyes glassy. "All sorts of stuff. They think no one's listening, but I hear 'em talking 'bout deals, shipments ... things moving in and out of town."

"What kind of shipments?"

"Dunno exactly," the drunk slurred. "Just know it's important. Big money stuff. Hennessey's boys don't mess around with small-time deals."

"Did they mention any names?" Jack pressed. "People they work with, places they go?"

The drunk squinted. "Heard 'em talk 'bout a guy named Joe. And there's some place in the old warehouse district they keep mentioning. Think that's where they move the goods."

Joe. The warehouse district. These were pieces Jack could use. "What about Lacy? What did they say about her?"

The drunk chuckled, a sound that turned into a cough. "Not much, just that she knows more than she lets on. Heard one of 'em say she's got her own secrets. But don't trust a drunk, right?"

Jack didn't know whether to trust the information, but it was better than nothing. He needed to follow up on these leads and find out what Lacy might be hiding.

Before he could ask more, the cell door clanged open, and a cop motioned for him to follow. "Noble, it's time for your interrogation."

Jack needed to get out of there. He needed to find Reese. Needed to figure out what this deal was. But first, he had to deal with Tilley.

"Noble, let's go," the cop said, motioning for Jack to stand.

He complied, his muscles stiff from sitting on the hard bench. The officer led him down the hallway to an interrogation room. A single overhead light illuminated the room. Tilley sat waiting, his expression unreadable.

"Have a seat, Jack." Tilley gestured to the chair opposite him.

Jack sat, his eyes locked on Tilley's. "What's this about?"

"You know damn well what this is about," Tilley said, leaning forward. "You've been poking around in things you shouldn't. Making a lot of powerful people very nervous."

"I'm trying to stop a man who's been killing and ruining lives," Jack said. "Is that what you're so worried about?"

Tilley clenched his jaw. "You've got it all wrong, Noble. You think you're the hero in this story, but you're just a pawn. Christ, we all are. Hennessey's too powerful. You can't take him down on your own."

"Maybe I'm not alone," Jack said. "You know nothing about me."

"I know you're playing a dangerous game, and it'll get you

killed. Look at what happened to Mark and Ben. One's dead, the other missing. Look at Ron. What do you think is gonna happen to you? Hmm?" Tilley paused a beat, leaned back in his chair, wrapped his hands around the back of his head. "Now, tell me everything you know about Hennessey's operations."

Jack remained silent. He stared defiantly at Tilley. He knew better than to spill everything here.

"Suit yourself." Tilley stood. "Enjoy your stay." He motioned to the officers, who hauled Jack back to his cell.

Back in the holding cell, Jack couldn't sit still. The confined space felt even smaller with each passing minute. He paced from one end to the other, the rough cement floor scuffing the soles of his shoes. His mind churned, trying to piece together the information the drunk had given him. Joe, the warehouse district, and Lacy's possible secrets—it was a lot to digest. He needed to get out of there and act on these leads, but for now, he was trapped.

The hours dragged on, the monotony broken only by the occasional sound of footsteps in the hallway. Each time, Jack's hopes would rise, thinking someone might be coming for him, only to be dashed when the steps faded away. The small, barred window let in a thin sliver of daylight, marking the slow passage of time.

Jack's thoughts became more jumbled. He thought of Reese, alone and possibly in danger. He replayed their conversations in his mind, searching for any clues she might have left about where she was going. Her note felt like a lifeline and a chain, pulling him in different directions.

He continued to dwell on what the drunk had said. Joe and the warehouse district seemed like solid leads, but the mention of Lacy troubled him. She had helped him before, but could she be hiding something? The thought gnawed at him. He needed to find out what she knew and whether she was involved in Hennessey's operations.

Jack's pacing increased, his frustration mounting. The hours felt like days, the small cell becoming a pressure cooker for his anxiety. He knew he couldn't stay there much longer. He needed to get out, find Reese, and stop Hennessey.

Finally, the cell door creaked open once more. Tilley stood there. He looked pissed. "You've got a visitor, Noble."

Jack frowned. "A visitor?"

"Follow me," Tilley said, not waiting for a response.

He led Jack down a series of corridors until they reached a small room. Tilley opened the door, and Jack stepped inside. His heart skipped a beat when he saw the man waiting for him.

"Hello, old friend. I've waited for this moment for a long time."

PART 3

CHAPTER 25

Marcus Wade sat calmly at the metal table, hands folded. He stood up as Jack was pushed into the chair opposite him. "Good to see you, Jack." His voice was almost too casual given the circumstances.

Jack glared at him, the anger and mistrust clear in his eyes. "Cut the crap, Marcus. What the hell is going on?"

Marcus leaned back, a small smile playing on his lips. "Straight to the point. I always liked that about you, Jack. Let's get one thing clear, Tilley is working for me, *not* Hennessey."

"You expect me to believe that? Tilley's been on Hennessey's payroll for years."

"True," Marcus said. "But he switched sides when he realized Hennessey was part of something much bigger. Something that needed to be stopped."

"And what exactly is this 'something'?"

Marcus's expression turned serious. "Hennessey isn't just a small-town crook. You've probably gathered that by now. He's part of a larger criminal network that stretches far beyond Lewiston. We're talking about drug trafficking, money laundering, and arms deals. The whole operation is intricate and deeply rooted.

Bringing down Hennessey alone won't solve the problem. We need to dismantle the entire network."

Jack rubbed the marks left behind on his wrist. "What is this we shit? Why should I trust you? Last time we worked together, you tried to kill me after I got you out of that prison in Afghanistan."

Marcus's jaw clenched at the mention of their past. "I won't deny our mistakes. But this isn't about us. This is about stopping a criminal empire that's ruining lives and corrupting institutions. We can't do it alone. We need each other."

Jack shoved his anger down. Marcus appeared sincere. "So, what's your plan?"

Marcus pulled out a folder and slid it across the table to Jack. "I've been gathering intelligence on the network for months. This folder contains details about their operations, key players, and weak points. We hit them hard, gather the evidence, and expose them. It's the only way to bring them down for good."

Jack glanced at the folder, then back at Marcus. "If I agree to this, it's only because I want Hennessey and whoever he's working with taken down. This doesn't mean I trust you."

Marcus nodded. "Fair enough. But know this, Jack, the moment we hesitate or let personal grudges get in the way, we lose. We can't afford that."

Jack picked up the folder, feeling the weight of the task ahead. The room pressed in on him. This alliance was fragile, built on a foundation of necessity rather than trust. Was he willing to take on that risk?

Jack flipped through the folder Marcus had given him. He remained skeptical. The betrayal in Afghanistan was still fresh in his mind, a wound that hadn't healed with time. He looked up at Marcus. "Why now? Why come to me? What's in it for you?"

Marcus leaned back in his chair, the faint hum of the overhead lights the only sound in the room. "Jack, I get it. You have every reason not to trust me. It's the same for me, man. But this isn't about us. This network is like a cancer, spreading through everything it touches. I need someone who can get things done, someone who understands the stakes. And like it or not, that's you."

Jack scoffed. "And I'm supposed to believe you're doing this out of the goodness of your heart? What's your angle, Marcus? You don't make moves without a reason."

Marcus's expression hardened. "You're right. I don't. But this isn't just about me. Yes, I have my reasons. I want redemption for my past mistakes, to make things right. And taking down this network will do that. But I also know that I can't do it alone. We've got a shared history, and despite everything, I know what you're capable of. We need each other to pull this off."

Jack studied Marcus, searching for any hint of deceit. Tension hung in the air between them. "This alliance is temporary, Marcus. I'm doing this for the greater good, not for you. The moment I sense any double-crossing, it's over."

Marcus nodded. "Understood. We're both walking a tightrope here, and I know the stakes. Let's set some ground rules. We communicate openly, no secrets. We verify everything we can. And we watch each other's backs. Agreed?"

Jack hesitated, then slowly extended his hand. "Agreed. But remember, Marcus, this truce is fragile. One wrong move, and it's done."

Marcus took Jack's hand, the handshake firm but wary. "Deal. Let's get out of here and get to work."

The truce was tenuous, a thin thread connecting two men with a complicated past. But with the stakes so high, they both knew that working together was their best chance at bringing down the network.

. . .

IN A SMALL HOUSE JUST OUTSIDE OF TOWN, MARCUS SPREAD A series of documents, maps, and photos across a dining table, each one a piece of a larger puzzle. Jack studied the array before him, the sheer scope of the network both daunting and eye-opening.

"These are the key players," Marcus said, pointing to a cluster of photos connected by lines on the map. "Hennessey is just one piece. The real power lies in the network—drug traffickers, money launderers, corrupt officials. They've built a web that extends far beyond Lewiston."

Jack focused on the faces and names. "So, we're not just dealing with Hennessey. We need to hit the entire network to bring them down."

"Exactly," Marcus said. "But we can't go after everyone at once. We need to find the weak points, the places where we can cause the most disruption and gather the evidence we need."

They spent the next hour identifying those weak points. Marcus highlighted a few key operations: a warehouse used for drug distribution, a shell company laundering money through legitimate businesses, and a corrupt politician who acted as a liaison between the network and law enforcement.

"This warehouse," Jack said, tapping one of the photos. "It's heavily guarded, but if we can get in and plant surveillance, we might be able to gather enough evidence to take it down."

Marcus nodded. "And the shell company. We need to trace the money, find out who's involved and how it's being moved. That's where you come in. You're good in the field, getting into places others can't. I'll handle the intelligence, coordination, and making sure we stay one step ahead."

Jack agreed, the division of roles clear. "I'll need surveillance equipment, secure communication channels, and a list of contacts who can help us on the ground."

Marcus opened a metal case, revealing an array of high-tech gadgets—miniature cameras, audio bugs, encrypted phones. "I've got you covered. Use these to gather intel. We'll set up a secure line so we can communicate without being intercepted."

They set clear objectives and timelines, planning their moves with precision. The first objective was to infiltrate the warehouse, plant the surveillance equipment, and monitor the activities inside. The second was to trace the money through the shell company, gathering evidence that could link it to the larger network. The third was to expose the corrupt politician, using the information to turn him against Hennessey and the network.

It all seemed so simple. The plan was set. They only had to execute. For the first time in a few hours, Jack thought of Reese and how helpful she would be to the operation. Ben, too.

Marcus stared at Jack for several seconds. "We're in this together now. Whatever our past differences, we have a common goal. Let's make sure we see this through."

"We will. For Brenda, for Reese, for Ben, and for everyone who's been hurt by these bastards."

CHAPTER 26

JACK SAT AT THE SMALL TABLE IN HIS HOTEL ROOM, THE surveillance equipment spread out before him. The tools Marcus had provided were impressive—miniature cameras that would blend in with the wall, audio bugs, and a high-tech encrypted phone. He double-checked each piece, ensuring everything was in working order.

Jack reviewed the plan Marcus had outlined, memorizing every detail. The warehouse was heavily guarded, with multiple entry points, rotating guard shifts, and a sophisticated security system. He had to be meticulous. One mistake could cost him everything. He folded the map of the warehouse and tucked it into his jacket pocket, then carefully packed the surveillance equipment into a small backpack.

Before departing, he went down to the lobby and found Sam behind the bar.

"Got any coffee brewed?" Jack asked.

"What? No bourbon?" Sam offered a smile.

"Not that kind of night. Soon, though. I'm sure."

"I hope so." Sam turned and filled a mug to the brim. "Cream? Sugar?"

"Black is fine."

"You hear from Reese?"

Jack shook his head. "She's smart getting out of here. This situation is far bigger than I ever could've imagined."

"Best you wish you had just driven on through town now."

"I end up where I'm supposed to end up. Always been that way. Figure it always will."

"I hope after this is finished, you end up in a place with sand and cocktails."

"I'll drink to that later."

As the sun began to set, Jack left the hotel and drove toward the warehouse district. The streets were quiet, the industrial area deserted at this hour. He parked a few blocks away and continued on foot, moving silently through the shadows. The air was crisp, the distant hum of machinery the only sound breaking the stillness.

Jack approached the warehouse from the rear, staying hidden behind a row of abandoned crates and pallets. He observed the guards, noting their patterns and shifts. They looked more like loggers, dressed in jeans and flannels. He couldn't tell if they were armed, but presumed they were. Two guards patrolled the perimeter in opposite directions. Their routes overlapped briefly at the northeast corner. A security camera panned slowly from side to side above the main entrance, and a secondary camera covered the rear loading dock.

He timed the guards' movements, noting a brief window when both were at the farthest points of their patrols. The cameras, he realized, had a blind spot at the rear entrance—just large enough for him to slip through if he moved quickly and precisely. Satisfied with his reconnaissance, Jack retreated to his hiding spot behind the crates and waited for the right moment.

When the guards were both at the far ends of their patrol routes, Jack stayed low, hugging the shadows, and made his way to the rear entrance. He reached into his backpack and pulled out a small device, which he used to disable the security camera temporarily. The camera's light blinked off, and Jack slipped inside.

The interior of the warehouse was dimly lit, the air thick with the smell of oil and metal. Stacks of crates and pallets created a maze of narrow corridors. Jack moved silently, his footsteps barely making a sound on the concrete floor. He carefully planted the surveillance cameras in strategic locations, ensuring they covered the main areas of activity. He placed audio bugs in areas where conversations were likely to occur, then made his way to the main office, where he installed the last of the devices.

With all of the equipment in place, Jack checked his watch. He needed to get out before the guards completed their next round. As he retraced his steps, he heard voices approaching. His pulse quickened. He ducked behind a stack of crates, holding his breath as two men passed by, their conversation a low murmur. He couldn't make out what they were saying. Once they were out of sight, Jack continued to the rear entrance.

He slipped out of the warehouse just as the security camera's light blinked back on. The night air was a welcome relief after the stuffy interior. It chilled the sweat on his forehead. He retraced his steps, keeping out of sight until he was safely back at his car. He took a deep breath, his heart still racing from the close call with the men inside. The first part of the mission was complete.

Jack was about to drive back to the hotel when his phone buzzed. He glanced at the screen, seeing an unknown number. His heart skipped a beat as he answered.

Jack's grip tightened on the steering wheel as Reese's voice came through the line, a mixture of urgency and relief. "Jack, I need to see you. We need to talk."

His pulse pounded. "Reese? Where are you?"

"I'm back in town. I know I said I was leaving, and I did, but I got a call from Ben. He's in hiding but wants to meet with us. He thinks we can take Hennessey down together."

"Why didn't you tell me you were coming back?"

"I didn't know who I could trust. And it's not that I can't trust you. I know I can. But I had to make sure Ben was safe first. Look, there's a lot to talk about. Can you meet me at the hotel?"

Jack took a deep breath. "I'll be there in ten minutes. Stay safe, Reese."

"I will. See you soon," she said, ending the call.

Jack put the Jeep in gear and drove toward the hotel. He'd hoped to take some time and come down from the adrenaline rush of infiltrating the warehouse. Still, he was happy to hear from Reese. Her return brought hope, but also increased the danger. He needed to stay sharp and figure out their next move.

When Jack arrived at the hotel, he parked the Jeep and hurried inside. He found Reese waiting in the lobby. As soon as she saw him, she rushed over and wrapped her arms around him, held him tight. Jack felt a surge of relief was over him.

"Reese, thank God you're okay," he said, pulling back slightly to look at her.

"I couldn't stay away," she said. "Ben called me. He escaped and found a safe place to hide, but he needs our help. He thinks we can bring down Hennessey's entire operation."

Jack led her to a quiet corner of the lobby. "Tell me everything."

Reese took a deep breath. "Ben managed to get away after the accident. He's been hiding out, trying to gather information. He found out that Hennessey is planning something big, and he believes we can expose him if we work together. He wants to meet us tonight."

"Where is he hiding?"

"An old cabin in the woods, not far from here. He says it's secure, but we need to be careful. Hennessey's men are everywhere."

"How many old cabins does this guy have?"

Reese smiled. "A lot, apparently."

Jack considered their options. His mind raced through various scenarios. He thought about the possible traps Hennessey's men could set, the ambushes they might face, and the potential for betrayal. Every step had to be calculated, every move precise. They couldn't afford any mistakes. Reese's safety weighed heavily on his mind, and he couldn't shake the nagging fear that Ben's information might lead them straight into danger. But the possibility of taking down Hennessey and his network was too important to ignore.

"We'll need to plan this carefully," Jack said. "We can't just walk into a trap."

Reese nodded. "I know. But Ben has information that could be crucial. We have to take the risk."

"Okay. We'll go tonight, leave in a few hours."

They spent the next few hours preparing for the meeting, reviewing their plans and gathering the necessary equipment.

Jack didn't mention Marcus or the uneasy alliance they had formed. He couldn't afford to reveal that card yet, not until he was sure he could trust Marcus—and he wasn't sure if that day would ever come. Their complicated past hung over him like a dark cloud, and the possibility of betrayal was always in the back of his mind.

Jack was also concerned about Ben. He wanted to believe that Ben's information was legitimate, but the danger of a setup loomed large. He glanced at Reese, grateful for her presence. She was the only one he felt he could trust completely in this tangled web of deceit and danger.

But the thought of one of the three—Ben, Reese, or Marcus—double-crossing him gnawed at his thoughts. He had to stay vigilant, keep his cards close, and ensure he wasn't being played from any angle.

CHAPTER 27

JACK NAVIGATED THE JEEP THROUGH THE WINDING FOREST road, the dense trees forming a dark canopy overhead. The headlights cut through the early morning fog that seemed to dance around them. He glanced over at Reese, who was scanning their surroundings. They had driven for miles, taking an extended route to ensure they weren't followed.

They barely spoke on the drive over. Jack had his concerns. Reese did as well. But they both wanted to give Ben the chance to convince them he was still on their side.

As they approached the cabin, Jack slowed down and turned off the headlights. They coasted the final stretch in silence, the only sound the crunch of gravel under the tires. He parked the Jeep behind a thicket of trees, well out of sight from any potential onlookers. Not that he expected any out here.

"Ready?" Jack asked.

Reese nodded. "Let's go."

They stepped out of the Jeep and made their way to the cabin. Jack was on high alert for any sign of trouble. The cabin was small and unassuming, almost blending into the surrounding forest. Jack knocked on the door in a specific pattern, and after a moment, it creaked open.

Ben stood in the doorway, looking worn and haggard but very much alive. His face lit up with relief at the sight of them. "You made it."

Reese enveloped Ben in a tight hug. "I'm so glad you're okay, Ben. The thought that something had happened to you..."

Ben hugged her back. It seemed to drain him of his remaining energy.

Jack closed the door behind them. He cast a quick glance around the room. The cabin was sparsely furnished, with only the essentials: a table, a few chairs, and a small cot in the corner. Maps and documents were spread out on the table, evidence of Ben's continued efforts to piece together Hennessey's network.

"We don't have much time." Ben led them to the table. "I've gathered as much information as I could while staying under the radar."

"Tell us everything," Jack said as he took a seat.

"After the accident, I knew I couldn't stay at the hospital," Ben said. "Hennessey's men were everywhere. I managed to slip away during the chaos and found a place to hide in the hospital. A quick change of clothes into scrubs, and I waltzed right out. I've been moving from place to place, trying to stay ahead of them, and got myself out here."

"I didn't see another vehicle," Jack said.

Ben waved him off and took a deep breath. He winced before exhaling. "I've been gathering intel on Hennessey's operations, trying to figure out his next move. We already know he's planning something big, but this is something that could solidify his power and make him untouchable. We have to stop him before it's too late."

Reese listened intently, her eyes filled with concern. "What's his plan?"

Ben spread out a map on the table, pointing to several marked locations. "Hennessey has been using the development project as a front for his real operations. He's been laundering money through shell companies, using legitimate businesses to cover his tracks. He's got connections in law enforcement, local government, even the state legislature. It's a web of corruption that runs deep."

Jack leaned forward, studying the map. "And you think we can bring him down?"

"We have to," Ben said. "But we can't do it alone. We need more evidence, more allies. I've identified key players in his network, people who can help us if we can convince them to turn against Hennessey."

Jack nodded. He already had one of them in Marcus, possibly.

They combined their findings, using maps, documents, and notes to create a comprehensive picture of Hennessey's operations. Jack pointed to a cluster of locations on the map.

"These are all connected to the shell companies we've identified. They're laundering money through fake construction projects, consulting firms, and other fronts."

Ben added his notes to the map. "Exactly. And here, these are the key businesses and people involved. We've got legitimate companies mixed in with Hennessey's operations, making it harder to trace the illegal activities. Some of these folks are good people. I can vouch for them. I'm positive they believe things are on the up and up."

"And once they find out it's not?" Jack said. "Will they side with us?"

Ben shrugged. "Can only hope so."

Reese pointed to one of the documents. "Look at this. These politicians and officials are all linked to Hennessey's front companies. He's got influence in places we didn't even realize."

They turned their attention to identifying the key players in the network. Ben pointed to a list of names. "These are the people we need to focus on. Corrupt officials, business associates, enforcers. They're the ones keeping Hennessey's operation running smoothly."

Reese nodded. "If we can take them down or turn them against Hennessey, we can start to dismantle his network from the inside."

Jack's mind was already at work on how to approach each target. "We need to find their vulnerabilities. Everyone has a weakness we can exploit. It's just a matter of figuring out what they are."

They discussed the vulnerabilities of these key players, brainstorming ways to gather more evidence or disrupt their operations. Some had financial weaknesses, others had personal secrets that could be used against them.

Reese pointed to one name on the list. "This guy, Councilman Harris. He's been involved in some shady deals, but he's got a clean public image. If we can expose his corruption, I bet we can get him to flip. It would be a huge blow to Hennessey's network."

Jack nodded. "Let's start there. What do you know about him, Ben?"

Ben sat back and smiled. "Practically raised the son of a bitch when I came back from New York. He was friends with my son. He was shady back then, too. I've always had my suspicions about him."

"What's our best plan of attack?"

"Head on, I'd say." Ben placed his index finger on the map. "That's his house. Reckon if we get there in the next hour, we can catch him."

"Let's get moving then." Jack felt his phone buzz against his thigh. He nodded at Reese. "Help him out." Then he hurried outside. He pulled his phone out and looked at the screen.

Marcus Wade.

CHAPTER 28

THE FOG BEGAN TO LIFT AS THE EARLY MORNING SUNLIGHT filtered through the dense trees surrounding the cabin. The air was crisp, carrying the fresh scent of pine and damp earth. Taking a deep breath, he answered the call.

"Noble." Marcus's voice came through the line, steady and serious. "I have something for you."

Jack decided to throw the Harris information out there. "So do I. What do you know about Councilman Harris?"

Marcus didn't even wait a beat. "Harris has been laundering money through a series of shell companies linked to Hennessey's operations. We've got financial records, emails, and a few recordings that tie him directly to the network. But he's slippery. He's got a clean public image, so you need to corner him with irrefutable evidence."

"Got it. Any advice on how to handle him? And what can you send me that will shake him up?"

"I do and will send it in a moment. Go in hard. He'll deny everything at first, but once you start presenting the evidence, he'll crack. Focus on the financial records and emails. They're the strongest pieces of evidence we have. And be prepared for anything. He might try to run, or worse, he might get desperate."

Jack's grip tightened on the phone. "Understood. We're heading there now."

"One more thing," Marcus added. "Keep an eye on Reese and Ben. Trust is in short supply right now, and we can't afford any mistakes."

Of the three—Reese, Ben, and Marcus—Marcus was the one he trusted least. "I know. We'll get it done."

Marcus ended the call without another word.

Jack slipped the phone back into his pocket and turned to help Ben out of the cabin. Together, he and Reese got Ben in the Jeep and they set off.

As they drove towards Councilman Harris' house, the forest gave way to suburban streets. The houses here were larger than the ones closer to town. Each one was a testament to the wealth and influence of its occupants. Harris' house was no exception—a sprawling two-story home with a well-maintained lawn and extra touches that spoke of affluence.

Jack parked a few houses down, out of sight from Harris' windows. They approached on foot. The lawns were wide and empty of trees and offered little cover. Jack felt the adrenaline coursing through his veins.

"Ready?" Jack asked.

"No better time than now," Reese said.

They walked up to the front door, their footsteps almost silent on the stone pathway. Jack knocked firmly, the sound echoing in the quiet morning. There was a long pause before they heard movement inside.

The door opened to reveal Councilman Frank Harris. His expression shifted from curiosity to nervousness as he recognized Ben. Perhaps he had been expecting the paperboy or the milk man.

"Ben, what's going on?" he asked. His eyes darted between the trio.

"We need to talk." Jack pushed the door open farther and stepped inside.

Harris tried to stop him but had no chance. "Talk about what?"

"About your involvement with Hennessey." Jack glanced around the foyer which led to a great room with a long island down the middle. Couches and TV on one side, kitchen on the other.

Harris took a step back in an attempt to place himself between Jack and the rest of the house. His eyes roamed all around the room as if looking for an escape route. "I don't know what you're talking about."

"Yeah, sure you don't." Jack nodded at Reese.

Reese stepped forward. She held up a folder filled with documents. "We have evidence, Councilman. Financial records, emails, recordings. All linking you to Hennessey's operations."

Harris' face paled as he glanced at the folder. "This is ridiculous. You have no proof. I'm a respected member of this community." He glared at Ben. "Ben, you know me. You know I would never do anything illegal. Tell these assholes you know that."

Ben shrugged as he walked past Harris. "You've always been a little shit, Frank."

Jack moved closer. "Respected or not, you're involved. And it's time you came clean."

Harris shook his head, his denial growing more desperate. "You're making a mistake. I have nothing to do with this."

Reese opened the folder and began laying out the evidence on a nearby table. "We have detailed records of your financial transactions, emails discussing laundering money through shell companies." She opened her phone and placed it in front of him. "And we even recordings of your conversations. There's no point in denying it anymore."

Harris slumped in his chair as he saw the evidence. His hands trembled as he set them on the table. "This ... this isn't what it looks like."

Jack leaned in and stuck his finger in the guy's face. "It's exactly what it looks like. You were bought off. Made a deal with the devil good for as long as he has a use for you. Pretty soon, the only use he'll have is to bury you. You're going to cooperate with us, or we'll make sure every detail of your involvement goes public. You'll lose everything. This house. Your family. Your job. Your power. Everything you've *worked* for will be gone. How does that sit with you?"

Harris said nothing.

"You were raised better than this," Ben said. "I don't know where things went wrong with you. But this isn't how you were taught to conduct yourself. Hell, I remember how excited you were for this position. How it was going to lead to better things for the town and for you. How you wanted to ride this into the state legislature, maybe even be governor one day. The hell happened, Frank?"

"Once you get in with Hennessey," Haris said. "There's no getting out. It started small. A favor. He came to me, said he could help me out. It wasn't anything big, but I was young and inexperienced in this position. I hadn't learned the importance of patience, that sometimes you have to negotiate a little bit to get what you want. He promised he could get it done, and he did. Then I found out his help comes with strings. He does you a favor, you do one for him. And then he just starts butting in, taking over. Taking more and more from you. You try to get out, and you receive threats against your family. So, you do what he says. And once you start digging that well, it just goes deeper and deeper until it's your body found in there."

"Is that what happened to Brenda?" Jack said.

"Her conviction is what happened to her. She should've backed off. If she had, she'd be alive now."

"Who did it?"

Harris shrugged. "I'm not privy to any of that information. Might as well assume any and all of them." He buried his face in his hands. "I wish I never fell in with these people. I just couldn't worm my way out."

"And I'm sure you got nothing for your trouble these past few years," Jack said.

Harris shook his head. "It's not like that. Yeah, he pays me, but I can't just walk away." He looked across the room where family photos adorned the mantle. "I've got a family. He'd have no problem making sure they disappear. I mean, look at what happened in the hospital the other night."

"What do you know about that?" Jack asked.

"Nothing, really. But it's obvious. He disposed of Mark and probably would have done the same to Ben had he not disappeared in the chaos."

"How do you know about how it all went down?" Reese asked.

Harris swallowed hard. He opened his mouth to speak, but before he could say anything, a gunshot rang out from outside the house, shattering the sliding glass door ten feet from them.

Jack, Reese, and Ben dropped to the floor. Another shot rang out. Jack's heart pounded. He crawled to the nearest window, pistol in hand, and peered out to see if he could spot the shooter. The sound of the gunshot echoed in his ears. Bushes set at the edge of the property rattled.

"Everyone stay down. Find cover. I'm going out."

"Jack," Reese said.

"What?"

"Look."

Jack turned his head and saw Harris on the floor, unmoving, in a puddle of his own blood.

CHAPTER 29

JACK BURST THROUGH THE DOOR AND INTO THE YARD, HIS heart pounding as he spotted the shooter through the bushes sprinting away. The shooter glanced back, his face hidden by a mask. He picked up speed, darted around the side of the house and into the neighboring yard. Jack didn't hesitate. He sprinted after him, his adrenaline pumping.

The shooter moved quickly, weaving through backyards, dodging between trees, and leaping over low fences. Jack followed, his breath coming in sharp bursts as he pushed himself to keep up. He barely avoided tripping over a garden gnome. He vaulted over a wooden fence just in time to see the shooter disappear around the corner of another house.

Jack's legs burned with the effort, but he kept his eyes locked on his target. The chase took them through a narrow alley, where trash cans and discarded furniture created a minefield of obstacles. The shooter knocked over a stack of boxes, trying to slow Jack down, but he agilely navigated through the debris, never losing sight of the fleeing man.

As they burst into the next yard, Jack saw the shooter head straight for a house. The guy threw open the back door and barged inside. Jack followed without a second thought. He slammed through the door and into the kitchen. A woman screamed and dropped a bowl of cereal as she saw the two men tear through her home.

"Sorry!" Jack shouted as he raced through the kitchen, the living room, and up the stairs after the shooter. The homeowner's confused shouts faded behind him as he focused on closing the distance between him and his target.

The chase continued up and down narrow hallways, through bedrooms and bathrooms, the two men barely avoiding crashing into walls and furniture. Jack could hear the panicked breathing of the shooter just ahead, and he pushed himself harder, determined to close the gap.

As they rounded a corner, Jack briefly lost sight of the guy. He heard a crash from the next room and charged forward, but as he entered, he saw no one. He paused, scanned the room, his senses on high alert. That's when he felt a sharp pain explode at the back of his head. The shooter had been waiting behind the door and had swung a heavy lamp with all his might.

Jack stumbled forward, his vision blurred from the impact. He barely managed to catch himself on the edge of a dresser. He fought against the black edges surrounding his vision. His mind reeled. The shooter bolted from his hiding spot, throwing a shoulder into Jack and then heading for the stairs. Jack shook his head, trying to clear the stars from his eyes, and forced himself to give chase once more.

The shooter's attempt to delay Jack had bought him precious seconds. Blood trickled down the back of Jack's neck, but he ignored it. The adrenaline pushed him forward. He burst out of the room, taking the stairs two at a time, and followed the shooter through the kitchen. The woman was on the phone and yelled at them that she was calling the police. Jack ignored her and ran out the back door.

He had regained his footing. They raced across the yard, and Jack saw the shooter head straight for a neighboring house. Without hesitation, the shooter kicked open the back door and barged inside, startling the family within. Jack was hot on his heels, apologizing quickly to the bewildered homeowners as he barreled through the kitchen and living room.

The chase took them up and down more narrow hallways, through bedrooms and bathrooms, the two men barely avoiding crashing into walls and furniture. The shooter threw obstacles in his path—chairs, lamps, anything he could get his hands on—but Jack navigated through the chaos.

As they burst out onto a balcony, the shooter leaped off the edge, landing in the backyard below with a grunt. Jack followed, ignoring the pain in his head and legs as he landed and rolled to absorb the impact. He was close now, so close he could almost reach out and grab the man. But when Jack went to stand, his left leg gave out and he crashed the ground. He felt his lower leg for a break. It didn't seem like anything had fractured, but the pain in his ankle was severe.

The shooter, limping slightly from the fall, pushed through the yard and back into the street. Jack forced himself off the ground. He staggered forward, his ankle loosening up every few steps. He closed the distance, determined not to let the guy escape. They were nearing the edge of the neighborhood, where a thick line of trees marked the beginning of a wooded area.

Just as the shooter reached the tree line, Jack saw his chance. He raised his pistol and fired, grazing the shooter's leg. The man cried out, clutching his wound but not stopping. He continued to limp away, each step more labored than the last. Jack could see the blood seeping through the fabric of the shooter's pants, leaving a trail of crimson droplets on the ground. The shooter's pace slowed. His movements grew more frantic and desperate. He stumbled over a fallen branch but managed to stay on his feet.

"Stop!" Jack shouted, his voice echoing through the trees. But the shooter, presumably driven by fear and adrenaline, pressed on, his breath coming in ragged gasps. Jack surged forward, closing the gap between them with every hobbled stride. The trees closed in around them, the dense foliage making it harder for them both to navigate.

Jack pressed on. Branches whipped at his face, leaving stinging cuts across his cheeks, but he didn't slow down. The underbrush tugged at his legs, threatening to trip him with every step. He ignored the pain in his busted ankle, gritting his teeth as he pushed through the dense foliage. Each step sent a jolt of agony up his leg, but he kept his focus on the shooter, who was now just a few yards ahead.

The shooter glanced back, his eyes wide with panic. Jack could see the man's desperation, the realization that he was losing ground. Jack surged forward. He could almost reach out and grab the shooter, the distance between them narrowing with every stride. He reached for his pistol and discovered it wasn't there.

Shit!

He'd have to take the guy down with force. But then, just as he was about to close the gap, Jack's foot caught on a hidden root. His ankle twisted painfully, sending him crashing to the ground. He let out a grunt of pain. He clutched his ankle as he tried to regain his footing. The shooter took advantage of Jack's fall and limped farther away.

Jack cursed under his breath and forced himself to stand despite the throbbing pain. He staggered forward, but the distance between him and the shooter had widened once more. The man was disappearing into the thick underbrush, his figure becoming a shadow among the trees.

Jack clawed his way forward. He used the trees to steady himself and keep upright. His fingers dug into the rough bark, pulling himself along as his ankle protested with every step. He gritted his teeth and refused to let the pain slow him down. The dense foliage tore at his clothes, but he pressed on, his eyes locked on the fleeting figure ahead.

Branches snapped underfoot, and the sound of his heavy breathing mingled with the rustling of leaves. Jack pushed through a particularly dense thicket, his hands and face scratched and bleeding, but he didn't care. The shooter was getting away, and he couldn't let that happen. He used every ounce of strength he had left, dragging himself forward, step by agonizing step.

Finally, he reached a small clearing, his lungs burning and his legs trembling from the effort. As they emerged from the woods, Jack saw the shooter stumble toward a hidden motorcycle. The man's movements were frantic, his hands shaking as he fumbled with the keys. Despite his injury, the shooter started it up and roared away, leaving Jack behind in a cloud of dust and frustration.

Breathing heavily, Jack watched helplessly as the shooter disappeared into the distance. He clenched his fists, the image of that tattoo burned into his mind. He had a lead, and he wasn't going to let this slip away.

CHAPTER 30

JACK LIMPED OUT OF THE WOODS, HIS BODY ACHING FROM THE chase. He re-tied his left hiking boot, making sure to pull it tight around his ankle to help keep the swelling down. He couldn't just rest for the next forty-eight hours. He'd have to power through.

The forest was quiet now, the only sounds the distant rustling of leaves and the soft chirping of birds. The air was cool, carrying the scent of pine and earth, mixed with the faint metallic tang of blood from the cuts on his face and hands.

He winced as he adjusted the boot, feeling the sharp throb of pain radiating from his twisted ankle. Sweat trickled down his forehead, mingling with the grime and blood from his earlier fall. He took a deep breath, the crisp air filling his lungs. He steadied himself. The sun rose higher. He let it wash over him before pulling out his phone. He dialed Reese's number, his fingers trembling slightly from the adrenaline.

"Jack?" Reese's voice was filled with concern.

"Yeah, it's me. I need you to come pick me up. I'm near the edge of the woods by Harris' place. The shooter got away, but I'm okay."

"Hang tight, we're on our way," Reese said.

Jack leaned against a tree, trying to steady his breathing. Within minutes, he could hear the distant hum of an engine as Reese and Ben approached in the Jeep. He straightened up, squinting against the glare of the morning sun, and walked toward the sound. Each step was a reminder of the grueling chase.

Reese rushed up to him. She threw an arm under his and helped him to the Jeep.

"Are you okay?" She looked him up and down, scanning his injuries.

"I'll live. Just a few scrapes and a twisted ankle." Jack winced as he put weight on his foot.

Ben helped him into the back seat of the Jeep. "We should get that looked at."

"I've survived far worse," Jack said. "Can't afford to take time away now. I'll keep it wrapped tight."

As they drove away from the woods, Jack pulled out his phone again and called Tilley.

"Tilley, it's Jack. We had a run-in with Councilman Harris."

"What happened?" Tilley asked, his voice tense.

"Harris is dead. We went there to confront him, get him to turn on Hennessey. A shooter ambushed us at his house and killed Tilley. I chased the guy through the neighborhood and into the woods, but he got away. I managed to get a good look at him. His face was concealed, but he had a tattoo, a distinctive one. We need to talk."

There was a pause on the other end. "Where are you now?"

"In the Jeep. Not sure where we're headed yet, but I'll let you know when we get there."

"Ten-four."

Jack disconnected the call and noticed Ben looking at him.

"Describe the tattoo," Ben said.

Jack leaned back in his seat. "It was a serpent coiled around a dagger. Lots of color. Color that didn't make sense for that piece. It was too bright. I know I've seen it before, but I can't place where."

Ben looked somber. "I've seen a lot of tattoos like that, Jack. Are you sure about it?"

Jack nodded.

"Reese," Ben said. "Take us to see Lacy."

As they reached the outskirts of town, they saw an ambulance and fire truck race by, accompanied by two police cars. Tilley drove one of them. He wondered if any of their evidence had been left behind. Wouldn't be the worst thing, he supposed. Tilley would take care of it, even if the other cops with him were bought off.

It was early, but the streets of downtown were lively, couples out for their morning walks and coffee. Kids on their way to school, which had reopened the day prior. Life went on as it did every day in Lewiston. Everyone either oblivious or uncaring about the evil undercurrent rushing through the town.

They arrived at Lacy's bar. The parking lot was empty. The sign turned off. The door locked. Ben pulled out his keyring and fished through the two-dozen or so keys it held. He slid one into the lock and turned it. Before pushing the door open, he looked back at Jack and Reese.

"I don't know how this will go down, so let's all be ready for anything."

Jack raised a finger. "Hang on a sec." He hobbled to the passenger side of the Jeep, reached in and opened the glove box. He retrieved the small Sig Sauer P938 9mm pistol he kept there. Not his first choice for a gunfight, but it was the perfect weapon for the bar should he need one.

Ben opened the door and held it as Jack limped inside, supported by Reese. The bar was empty. The usual smell of bison burger failed to greet them. Instead, it smelled like bleach and beer, an off-putting odor after what they'd already been through that morning.

Jack scanned the room in search of the piece of the puzzle he was missing.

Then he saw it. A framed photo behind the bar. It was Lacy with a young man, her son. The young man had a tattoo on his arm —a serpent coiled around a dagger.

The height, the build, the tattoo. It all matched the shooter and the mystery man at the hospital.

Ben walked over to the photo and took it off the wall. He shook his head as he stared down at it. He flipped it around and said, "Jack, is that the tattoo?"

Jack nodded. He thought about what to do next. Call Tilley? Marcus? Set out on their own to find Lacy's son?

Reese said, "We need to find him. Now."

"Find who?" Stepping out from the shadows of the hallway was Lacy. "What are you three doing in here?"

"Still got a key," Ben said.

"Remind me to get that back from you," Lacy said.

Jack took a step forward, his eyes locked on Lacy. He had his doubts about the woman. She seemed to be at the center of a lot of the things going on. "We need to talk about your son, Lacy."

Her expression hardened. "What about him?"

"We think he's involved with Hennessey," Jack said. "We've seen him at the hospital, and we believe he's the one who shot Councilman Harris this morning."

Lacy's expression dropped. "No. That can't be. Danny would never do something like that. He's a good kid. Hell, you've sat with him at this bar, Jack. All he does is joke around."

Jack pointed to the photo. "The tattoo, Lacy. I saw it on the man I chased this morning. It matches. Danny's mixed up in this, whether you want to believe it or not."

She shook her head. "You don't understand. Danny's been through a lot. He's made mistakes, but he's not a killer."

Ben stepped in. "Lacy, we need to know where he is. If he's in trouble, we can help him. But we need to find him first."

Lacy's eyes filled with tears. "You're wrong. He's not involved. He couldn't be."

"Lacy," Jack said, "we need to know what's going on. Where is he?"

She wiped her eyes and took a deep breath. "I don't know. I haven't seen him in days. He's been staying away ever since..."

"Ever since what?" Reese asked.

"Ever since he beat up Ron at the cabin," Lacy said, her voice breaking. "Ron was trying to convince him to stop working with Hennessey. Said it didn't matter what Hennessey had on them, they needed to get out. Danny didn't want to hear it. They fought, and Danny ... he lost control."

Jack exchanged a look with Reese and Ben. "We need to find him, Lacy. Do you have any idea where he might be hiding?"

She shook her head. "No, but he has a friend. They used to hang out at the old warehouse near the river. Maybe he's there."

Before they could respond, Ben's phone rang. He glanced at the screen. "It's Sam. Hold on." He answered the call. "Yeah, Sam, what's up?"

Ben's expression turned serious as he listened. "Hold on, Sam. What's wrong?" He listened intently for another moment. "We're on our way." He ended the call and turned to Jack and Reese, his face pale. "Sam's in trouble. We need to go, now."

Without another word, they rushed out of the bar and back into the Jeep.

CHAPTER 31

THE JEEP ROARED DOWN THE DESERTED STREETS, ITS TIRES screeching at every turn. Jack's knuckles were white as he gripped the steering wheel as his mind raced through the possible scenarios they might face. Beside him, Reese scanned the surroundings, her hand hovering near her pistol. Ben sat in the back, tense and alert, ready for whatever lay ahead.

The urgency in Ben's voice during the call had set their adrenaline pumping. They knew they were heading into a confrontation. Jack couldn't help wonder why Sam? He knew little about the man, but he didn't seem tied up in everything. Was this just a ploy to bring Jack to them? A way for them to guarantee uneven footing?

As they approached Sam's house, the first light of dawn cast a soft glow over the neighborhood. Jack slowed down. He looked for any signs of movement.

"There." Reese pointed to the front door, which hung ajar. The frame was splintered, evidence of a forced entry.

Jack parked the Jeep a few houses away. "This could get messy."

They exited the vehicle and crossed the distance as silently as they could. Jack led the way, signaling for Reese and Ben to follow closely. They stuck close to the neighboring houses to shield themselves from any lookouts. As they approached the house, the quietness heightened their tension. Jack nearly drew his sidearm when a nearby car started up.

They reached Sam's house. Jack peered through a side window. The living room was dimly lit. He could make out the figures of several men, and the faint sound of muffled voices reached his ears. He turned to Reese and Ben, nodding toward the front door.

"Ready?" Jack mouthed.

They both nodded in response.

Jack pushed the door open and winced at the creak it made. They slipped inside, moving through the darkened hallway with the kind of practiced stealth they had developed over years in the field. Each creak of the floorboards beneath their feet made his heart race faster.

The living room was close. The sound of a struggle became clearer. Jack held up his hand, signaling for them to stop. He peeked around the corner and took in the scene before him. Sam was tied to a chair in the center of the room, bruised and bloodied. Three of Hennessey's men surrounded him. They hovered over Sam like they were intent on extracting information. Or beating the crap out of him.

Jack's gaze hardened. He glanced back at Reese and Ben and signaled them to get ready. They needed to take out these men quickly and efficiently.

Jack stepped into the room, his pistol raised. "I'm the guy you want."

The men turned in surprise, but Jack didn't hesitate. He fired two quick shots, each one hitting its mark, center mass. The men crumpled to the floor. The third man lunged at Jack, but Reese was faster. She drew her weapon and fired, hitting him in the leg. He dropped with a scream, clutching his wound.

"Stay down!" Reese commanded, her gun trained on the injured man.

Jack moved to Sam. He pulled a knife and cut through the ropes binding the man. "Are you okay?"

Sam groaned, his head falling forward. "I've been better. But there's something you need to know ... about Hennessey's true identity...." His eyes fluttered and his voice trailed off as he lost consciousness.

"Shit," Jack said. They had come to rescue Sam, but it was clear their troubles were far from over. Jack turned back to the injured man on the floor, who was still clutching his leg and groaning in pain. "Who sent you?"

The man spat blood and glared at Jack. "You're too late. Hennessey knows everything. You're all dead."

Reese stepped forward, her gun still aimed at the man. "Wrong answer." She glanced at Jack, who nodded. They needed answers. They needed this guy alive.

Jack holstered his gun and moved to the man, grabbing him by the collar. "Who is Hennessey? Where can we find him?"

The man laughed, a harsh, grating sound. "You think you can stop him? You have no idea what you're up against."

Before Jack could react, the man made a sudden move, reaching for a knife hidden in his boot. Jack was faster. He brought the butt of his pistol down hard on the man's head, knocking him out cold.

"Damn it," Jack muttered, running a hand through his hair. "We needed him conscious." He glanced back at Sam. "How is he?

Reese knelt beside Sam and checked his pulse. "He's stable for now, but we need to get him out of here."

Ben was already at the door. He checked outside for backup.

"It's clear. We should move. We don't know if more of Hennessey's men are on the way."

Jack and Reese lifted Sam, supporting him between them as they made their way out of the house. Ben took the lead. His pistol followed his gaze.

The morning sun had crested the trees. Jack winced at the brightness.

They reached the Jeep and loaded Sam into the backseat.

"No loose ends," Reese said. "We need to go back and get the other guy."

Jack and Reese hurried back into the house. The living room was quiet, the only sound the ticking of a clock on the wall.

"He's gone." Jack searched for any sign of the wounded and saw a trail of blood leading out of the room. "He must've escaped through the back."

They rushed through the house, heading to the back door. It was slightly ajar, swinging gently in the breeze. Jack pushed it open and stepped outside. The backyard was empty, the fence gate wide open.

"He's gone," Reese said.

Jack cursed under his breath. "We can't waste any more time. Let's get back to Sam."

They returned to the Jeep. Jack took the wheel, his mind racing with the urgency of their situation. As they sped away, Jack glanced in the rearview mirror at Sam, who remained unconscious as he slumped against Ben. They needed answers, and they needed them fast. But first, they had to make sure Sam was safe. Then, they could figure out their next move.

"Ben," Jack said. "You ever met Hennessey?"

Ben shook his head. "Always been a mystery how this guy has so much power, yet no one ever sees him."

"So, what Sam said back there, about his true identity..."

"Been on my mind since he spoke it. When you think about

how things have gone, every turn a dead end, it's like someone knew exactly what we were doing before we even did it."

"My thoughts exactly," Jack said. He felt his phone buzz in his pocket. He pulled it out and saw a message from Marcus. "We need to talk. Urgent." He clenched his jaw. One more complication. He couldn't trust Marcus, but right now, they needed all the help they could get.

"We need to find a safe place for Sam," Jack said. "Then we're going to have a little chat with Marcus. It's time to get some answers."

The Jeep roared down the road, the tension inside the vehicle thick enough to cut with a knife. Jack knew they were getting closer to the truth, but the danger was far from over. They were heading into the heart of the storm, and they couldn't look back now.

CHAPTER 32

JACK KEPT HIS EYES ON THE REARVIEW MIRROR AS THEY SPED away from Sam's house. As they drove through the outskirts of town, he noticed a dark SUV gaining on them from a distance.

"We've got company," he said.

Reese twisted in her seat to get a better look. "They must've sent more men. We need to lose them."

Jack nodded. "Hold on, everyone."

He accelerated, and the Jeep's engine roared as they sped down the narrow, winding roads. The SUV closed in, its flashing high beams glaring in the rearview mirror. Jack swerved around a corner, the tires screeching as he maneuvered through the tight turns.

"Ben, make sure Sam's secure back there." Jack remained focused on the road ahead.

Ben held onto Sam, who remained unconscious, slumped against him.

Jack took another sharp turn, nearly missing a parked car. The SUV followed, relentless in its pursuit. He scanned the road ahead, looking for any opportunity to shake them off. Up ahead, he spotted a narrow dirt path leading into the woods.

"Hang on!" Jack veered onto the dirt path, slipping the Jeep into four-high.

The Jeep bounced over the rough terrain as the forest closed in around them. The dirt road turned into two slim patches of dirt and eventually into nothing at all. Branches scraped against the sides of the vehicle as they sped deeper into the woods. The SUV followed, its engine growling as it struggled to keep up.

"We need to create some distance," Reese said.

Jack nodded as he focused on the path ahead. He spotted a fallen tree partially blocking the path. He aimed the Jeep for a narrow gap beside the tree, praying they'd make it through.

The Jeep squeezed past, the side scraping against the rough bark, sending splinters flying. The metal groaned under the pressure, the tires kicking up dirt and debris as Jack wrestled with the wheel to keep them on course.

The SUV wasn't as fortunate. It slammed into the tree with a deafening crash, the impact sending the vehicle's front-end crumpling like an accordion. The force of the collision jarred the vehicle to a halt, its occupants thrown violently forward. Jack glanced in the rearview mirror, relieved to see their pursuers momentarily stopped as steam rose from the wreckage and the inhabitants scrambled to recover from the sudden stop. Two men exited the vehicle and gave chase on foot, but they gave up as the Jeep rolled forward.

"That should buy us some time," Jack said, his grip on the wheel easing.

They continued through the woods until Jack found a secluded spot and parked. The forest around them was dense and silent, providing the cover they needed. After a few minutes of downtime, they corrected course and made their way to the cabin.

Once there, they laid Sam on a cot in the corner of the main room. Reese set to work, cleaning his wounds and checking for any serious injuries. Ben stood guard by the window, keeping an eye out for any signs of pursuit.

Jack paced the room, his thoughts a jumbled mess. "We need to figure out our next move. If what Sam said is true, the dynamics of the threat and situation have changed, and not for the better."

Reese sat on the edge of a worn couch, her brow furrowed. "We can't trust anyone right now. We need to verify everything. Who knows how deep this goes?"

Ben leaned against the wall, his arms crossed. "Hennessey has been playing us from the start. Every move we've made, he's been one step ahead."

"Which means Marcus might be in on it too." Jack stopped to look at Ben. "He's been feeding us information, but how do we know it's not all part of their plan?"

Reese nodded. "It makes sense. From what you've told me, Marcus has always been slippery. We need to confront him, but we have to be smart about it. We can't let him know we're onto him until we have concrete evidence."

Jack rubbed his temples. "And we have to find Danny. He might be the key to bringing this whole thing down."

"But where do we start?" Ben asked. "The warehouse? The bar?"

Jack shook his head. "We need to be careful. If we make a wrong move, it could tip them off."

Reese looked at Sam, still unconscious on the bed. "When he wakes up, we'll get more information. Until then, we need to prepare for whatever comes next."

Jack nodded. "Agreed. Let's get ready."

Sam stirred, a low groan escaping his lips. Jack, Reese, and Ben moved closer, ready to hear what he had to say. His eyes fluttered open. He looked around, disoriented, before focusing on Jack. "Hennessey ... it's all a lie."

"Tell us everything, Sam." Jack knelt beside him and leaned in to hear better.

Sam took a shaky breath and winced in pain. "Hennessey isn't a person. It's a facade."

"How do you mean?"

"A stolen identity and a story created by Lacy, Ron, and Danny. They've been running the whole operation from behind the scenes. Well, mostly Lacy running things with the other two being the main muscle."

Reese's eyes widened in shock. "Lacy? Are you sure?"

"Do you have proof of this?" Ben asked. "I've known Lacy, well, as long as she's been alive."

Sam nodded weakly. "She's been manipulating everything. There's receipts. I only caught on recently, and it was by accident. I thought I covered my tracks, but obviously she knew."

"Where's this information?"

Sam shook his head. "They took it. Before you got there, they made me hand it over. It's in Lacy's possession, and I'm sure destroyed by now. And there's more. Marcus Wade. He's been playing both sides, feeding them information about our every move."

Jack clenched his fists. Anger rose like bile. "We need to confront Marcus. But first, we need to make sure we're ready. This changes everything."

Jack, Reese, and Ben gathered around the table to discuss the situation.

"Lacy, Ron, and Danny," Jack said. "I can't believe it."

Ben leaned forward. "I know them like they're my kin. I can't believe it either. But we need to use this information to our advantage. If we can expose them, we can take down the entire operation."

"How do we do that if they have all of Sam's evidence?" Reese asked.

"We see what we can get out of Marcus," Jack said. "If there's receipts, I have a feeling he'll have them. But we gotta be smart. He's dangerous. He knows how to cover his tracks."

"And he hates you." Reese smirked.

"Might be his only redeeming quality." Jack returned her smile.

"Let me handle Lacy," Ben said. "This betrayal, it cuts deep. I want to confront her."

"I don't know if that's the best idea," Jack said.

"I can do it," he said. "You two go deal with Marcus, and let me go to her like I'm none the wiser."

"But that third guy escaped the house," Reese said. "The men followed us, saw you with us and Sam. She'll know."

Ben leaned back, sighed, resigning himself that his idea wouldn't work.

"Let's have you initiate contact with her," Jack said. "Maybe she'll be willing to end this peacefully."

"I'll do that then," Ben said.

Jack glanced at his phone, the message from Marcus still displayed on the screen. "We'll set a trap. Use the information Sam gave us to lure Marcus out and get him to reveal his true intentions. His fate will rest on how willing he is to cooperate."

Jack's fingers flew over the phone's keyboard, crafting a message that would lure Marcus into a meeting. "Need intel ASAP. Meet behind the inn in one hour."

CHAPTER 33

REESE LOOKED OVER JACK'S SHOULDER AS HE SENT THE message. "Think he'll take the bait?"

"He will. Marcus is too deep in this to ignore a call for help. Question is whether he'll buy it. There's no way he trusts me. He shouldn't. I wouldn't. Maybe he's really working in some official capacity against Hennessey, but I have no doubt he's double dipping. He sees me as a pawn. Always has. He was never pissed he got left behind in Afghanistan. He was pissed he didn't leave me behind."

"So, what's the plan?" Reese asked. "We can't afford any mistakes here. If Marcus is as two-faced as we think, he'll be on high alert."

Jack rubbed his temples. "We need to catch him off guard. Make him think he's in control until we spring the trap. He's smart, but he's not infallible, even if he thinks he is. We use his ego to take him down."

Reese glanced at Ben. "You're our backup. If things go sideways, we need to be ready to act fast."

Ben secured his sidearm and checked the magazine. "We need to control every aspect of this meeting."

Jack agreed. "No room for error. I get him talking, get the information we need, and then we all move in. Marcus is dangerous, but we're not giving him any chances to outmaneuver us."

Ben unfolded a map and pointed at the inn's location. "Right here, Jack. That's where you should post up. I'll be on the right, Reese on the left. There's a dumpster she can take cover behind."

"Why do I get the dumpster?" Reese laughed.

Ben shrugged. "We can switch, if you want, but you'll be trading trash for a grease trap."

Jack walked over the fireplace. The burning embers offered a touch of warmth in the chilled room. "What about Sam? Think it's safe to just leave him here?"

"No," Ben said. "But we don't have much choice. He can't be with us. If we bring him to the inn in this shape, the night manager will call the cops. Half of them are on Hennessey's payroll, and it seems like the other half might be controlled by Marcus."

"So we risk him staying here," Jack said.

"I could stay behind," Ben said.

"Afraid that'll weaken us too much," Jack said.

"We should get going," Reese said. "Let's take our chances leaving Sam here."

"You all go ahead," Sam said. "Just leave me a pistol and I'll manage."

With that, they set out for town. Jack dropped Reese west of the inn, Ben to the east. Each had their designated position to post up. He'd have to trust that they would.

The Jeep's headlights washed over the rear parking lot Jack pulled in. There were a few cars behind the hotel. A few parked by the BBQ restaurant. The waitress from the night before leaned against the side of the restaurant, smoking a cigarette.

Jack cut the headlights and engine, coasted into a spot. He pulled the e-brake and took a moment to settle himself. The cool night air enveloped him. Even with the distance between him and the waitress, he caught a whiff of cigarette smoke. He ignored it. Let his mind relax until he saw how the meeting would play out.

Before exiting the Jeep, Jack adjusted his earpiece. He whispered, "Stay sharp. We don't know what Marcus might pull. Everyone ready?"

"In position," Reese said.

"Same," Ben said.

Jack stood behind the inn with his back against the cold brick wall. The rear entrance was twenty feet to his right. Muffled voices from those inside whispered on the breeze. Across the parking lot, smoke rose from the restaurant and melted into the dark sky. He casually looked left and right at Reese and Ben's positions. Even knowing they were there, he couldn't spot them. That bode well, unless Marcus had eyes on the location already.

The minutes ticked by, each one adding to the tension. Finally, headlights appeared. A black SUV turned into the parking lot, K-turned, and stopped facing the exit, ready for a quick getaway, presumably.

The driver's door opened and a man stepped out. He shuffled a few feet toward Jack and opened the rear door. Marcus appeared, his silhouette first framed by the dim streetlights, then by the red brake lights. The driver remained in position, by the door, his hands unseen.

There was a crackle in Jack's ear, and Ben came on the line. "Driver is mine."

Reese whispered, "There's some activity over here. As the SUV pulled up, another vehicle parked on the street out of sight from me."

Marcus walked halfway from the SUV to Jack and stopped. "What's going on, Jack? What's so important you needed to meet like this?"

Jack stepped forward. "We need to talk, Marcus. Things are getting out of hand."

Marcus approached slowly, his eyes darting around. He was tense. Jack had seen him like this before. Marcus was anticipating the deception.

"I've been trying to get in touch with you. What's happening?"

Jack subtly moved his hand, signaling to Reese and Ben that it was time. His goal was to get Marcus to start talking and move in once he clammed up.

"You tell me, Marcus. How deep are you in with Hennessey?"

Marcus smiled. "What are you talking about?"

Jack didn't let up. "We know who Hennessey really is. We know all about Lacy, Ron, and Danny. And we know you've been playing both sides."

Marcus scoffed. "You've got it all wrong, Jack. I've been trying to take them down from the inside. You know I've always been about the bigger picture. Christ, we went over this already."

Jack's eyes narrowed. "Is that so? Because it looks like you've been feeding them information about our every move. How do you explain that?"

Marcus's face tightened. "You have no idea what it's like, the things I've had to do to get close to them. Sacrifices had to be made. The end result is all I care about. If something happens to anyone involved, it's their fault for being involved."

Jack stepped closer. "Sacrifices? Like setting us up at Harris's place? You knew what would happen there. How many more people have to die because of your games?"

Marcus clenched his jaw. "You think it's that simple? You think I wanted any of this? You don't know the half of what I've been through, the risks I've taken."

The earpiece crackled. "Driver's getting antsy," Ben said.

Jack's voice was cold. "I don't care about your risks. I care about the lives you've put in danger, the people who've died because of your actions."

Marcus took a step back. "Jack, listen to me. If you take me down now, you lose your best chance at taking down Hennessey's operations for good. I've got connections, information you'll never get without me."

Jack hesitated. "Why should I trust you? Give me one good reason not to end this right here."

Marcus's eyes flickered with desperation. "Because I can give you Hennessey. I can give you Lacy, Ron, and Danny. But you have to let me help you."

Before Marcus could react, Reese and Ben stepped out of the shadows, their weapons drawn. Marcus froze, his hands instinctively raising in surrender.

"Easy, Jack," Marcus said. "Let's talk this through. There's more at play here than you realize."

"Start talking, then," Jack said. "And it better be good."

Reese and Ben moved in, disarming Marcus and the driver, then securing their hands with zip ties. The standoff ended as quickly as it had begun, with Marcus captured and restrained.

"You're making a huge mistake, Jack. We're wasting time here. Something big is about to go down, and it's just a couple blocks away."

"Cover them, Ben," Jack said. He pulled Reese to the side. "Check in the bar, see what it looks like. If Marcus is telling the truth, we might not want to waste time going back to the cabin."

"What if he has more people waiting? What about that car I heard pull up?"

"We'll take our chances that they think the hotel is too public."

"And if they don't?"

"Then we'll deal with it."

Reese nodded and disappeared inside. The seconds that passed felt like minutes. She pushed through the door and waved them forward.

"It's already shut down. We're good in there."

They made their way into the establishment. They led Marcus

and the driver behind the bar, into the kitchen. Emergency lighting lit the space up with a reddish glow. Ben escorted the driver to the refrigerator walk-in and locked him in there. The kitchen was far enough from prying eyes but close enough for a quick escape if needed.

They sat Marcus down on a worn chair. Jack leaned in. "Start talking, Marcus. How deep does this go?"

Marcus glanced around. "You don't understand. It's not as simple as you think."

Jack's patience was wearing thin. "Make us understand."

Marcus took a deep breath, regaining his composure. "Lacy, Ron, and Danny—they're the real power behind Hennessey. You're right about that. It's all a facade. They've been using the name to control everything. And yes, I've been helping them, but not because I had no choice."

Reese stepped up, towering over the seated man. She waited until he looked her in the eye. "Then why? What's your angle?"

Marcus's eyes hardened. "Power. Influence. You know as well as I do that playing by the rules doesn't get you anywhere in this game. Look at you, Reese. How many times has the FBI moved you? If you survive tonight, I guarantee that tomorrow there will be ten feds here, whisking you away to your next destination, if not a jail cell."

"Leave her out of this," Jack said.

"Screw you, Jack. I didn't get into this to play second fiddle. I've been positioning myself to take over."

Jack raised an eyebrow. "Take over? From the inside?"

Marcus nodded. "Exactly. I've been gathering intel, learning their weaknesses. I'm not their pawn. I'm biding my time. When the moment's right, I'll take them down and control the entire operation."

Ben stepped forward. "And we're supposed to believe you're on our side now?"

Marcus smirked. "I'm on *my* side, Ben. But our interests align. You want to bring them down? So do I. The difference is, I know how."

Reese looked skeptical. "And what's stopping us from taking you down right now?"

Marcus shrugged. "You could. But you won't get far without me. I know their plans, their operations. I can help you get to them. And I can help you do it tonight. And when they're out of the picture, we'll see who's left standing."

Jack's eyes narrowed. "And if we refuse your help?"

Marcus's smile faded. "Then you'll be walking blind into a trap. I'm offering you a chance to take them down from the inside. You don't have to trust me, but you need me."

"And what if we decide to take you out right after?"

"You won't."

"Why's that?"

A grin widened. His teeth glowed red. "Because if I don't call a certain number by six am tomorrow, your little girl will be whisked away from her dead uncle."

Jack lunged forward, drove a right hook into Marcus's face. The man toppled over, but Jack didn't stop. He slammed his foot into the guy's back and ribs.

"Jack!" Reese wrapped her arms around him and pulled back. "We can't do this. Even if he's bluffing, we can't do this."

Marcus's groans turned into laughter. He rolled over, still smiling. His teeth really were red now, covered in his blood. "That's the Jack I need tonight. Glad to see he still exists."

"If you hurt one hair on my girl's head—"

"Don't worry, old friend. Help me achieve what I'm here to do, and everything will be just fine."

CHAPTER 34

JACK PULLED THE JEEP TO A STOP A SAFE DISTANCE FROM Lacy's bar. The neon sign cast a faint glow on the pavement and a haze in the night sky, flickering as the last stragglers exited the bar, laughing and stumbling into the night. Were they aware of the deception within?

Jack cut the engine and turned to Reese, Marcus, and Ben. "We'll wait until it's completely empty. We go in quietly."

Reese checked her weapon. "Got it."

Marcus leaned back in his seat, staring out at the bar. He seemed tense. Jack couldn't get a read on the man. How much of what he had said was true? At the end of the day, if Jack had to put a bullet in the man's head, he had no qualms about it. If he intended to hurt Mia, he deserved to die. If he bluffed Jack about Mia in order to buy himself some time, he deserved to die.

Marcus looked up from the bar. "You know, I never thought it would come to this. Being here, working with you again."

Jack kept his eyes on the bar. "Why the hatred? What did I do that was so unforgivable?"

Marcus clenched his fists. "It wasn't just you, Jack. It was everything you represented. You came into the SIS like you owned the place. Frank Skinner's new golden boy. I'd been there for years, working my ass off, and suddenly you show up and take my spot."

Jack turned to face him. "You were a prisoner in Afghanistan, Marcus. We rescued you. That should have been enough to solidify my presence in the agency."

Marcus's eyes flashed with anger. "Enough? You think *that* was enough? You have no idea what it was like being in there, what I went through. And then to come back and see you in my place, succeeding where I had failed. It was like a slap in the face."

Jack's jaw tightened. "So, this is all because of your ego?"

Marcus looked away. "Maybe. Partly. But it's more than that. Every mission you completed, every accolade you received—it was because I had failed."

"That was years ago."

"Funny. Still feels like yesterday to me."

Jack shook his head. "And now? What do you hope to achieve with all this?"

Marcus met his gaze. "Control. Power. I want to take over. I've been positioning myself to take down Hennessey and his operation from the inside. When this is over, I'll be the one in charge. No more government officials controlling me. I'll have them in my pockets."

"And you think we're just gonna let that happen?"

Marcus smirked. "You need me, Jack." The smile from his face dropped. "And as much as I hate to admit it, we need each other right now."

"We don't need you at all."

Marcus jutted his chin to the left. "See that car there?"

Jack turned to look. Through the tinted windows he could make out two heads.

"Those are my guys," Marcus said. "They're insurance if this whole thing goes awry."

"The car I heard," Reese said.

Marcus nodded.

Jack turned back to the bar, the last patrons stumbling away. The neon sign flickered one last time before shutting off. The area fell into a darkness as the sign faded.

"Let's get this done." Jack opened his door and stepped out into the cool night air. The others followed suit.

They moved quickly and quietly, taking up their positions around the bar. Jack, Reese, and Marcus would enter together, while Ben kept watch outside, ready to provide backup if needed. Marcus's men remained in their vehicle. Jack wondered what their true purpose was, but shoved the question down. He couldn't worry about that now. The time would come, and he'd deal with it then.

Jack glanced at Marcus before they entered. "Stay close and follow my lead. No mistakes." He reached for the door, stopped, looked back again. "Don't fuck me over."

Marcus nodded. "Let's do this."

With that, they slipped inside, the door closing softly behind them. The bar was dark and silent, the only sound the faint hum of the refrigerator in the back. The smell of beer and bison burgers lingered. The floor felt sticky in spots.

They moved through the space, their footsteps muffled on the worn wooden floor.

In the back, they could hear voices, low and urgent. Jack signaled for them to stop. He listened, trying to make out what was being said. From what they could hear, it was clear that a big deal was going down.

Jack took a deep breath and nodded to Reese and Marcus. It was time to move.

He led the way. Reese was to his right. Marcus to his left. Every cell in his body was on high alert as they approached the back room. The voices grew louder and more distinct. There were multiple people behind the closed door. He held up his hand, signaling for Reese and Marcus to stop.

"...make sure the shipment is ready by morning. No mistakes this time," a gruff voice said.

Jack glanced at Reese and Marcus. "Ready?"

They both nodded. Jack took a deep breath, then kicked the door open. The room erupted into chaos. Several men turned. Danny and Ron were at the center, surrounded by four other men. Lacy stood near the back. It only took a second for the look on her face to change from confusion to anger.

"Freeze!" Jack shouted, his gun trained on a man with his pistol already at his side.

For a moment, time seemed to stand still. Then, all hell broke loose. One of the other men reached for his weapon, and Jack fired, hitting him in the chest. The guy dropped, but before Jack could pick another target, the room exploded into a frenzy of gunfire.

Jack and Reese moved in tandem. Neither had to direct the other. Their movements were synchronized as they overturned a table and took cover. Bullets whizzed past, shattering bottles and sending splinters of wood flying.

Marcus ducked behind a pillar. He returned fire. He grunted in pain as he took a bullet to his arm. It didn't stop him. He took out the second guy.

Jack hit another. The guy dropped to a knee. Reese finished him off.

Jack glanced over at Marcus. "You okay?" Not that he really cared.

Marcus nodded, wincing. "Just a scratch. Don't worry about me."

The gunfire continued, more sporadic than at first. The noise was deafening in the confined space. Jack spotted Danny trying to make a run for it and aimed his gun. "Stop, Danny!"

Danny ignored him and sprinted towards the exit. Jack fired, hitting him in the leg. Danny stumbled and fell, crying out in pain.

Ron roared in anger, firing wildly at Jack and Reese. "You'll pay for that!"

Jack ducked as bullets thudded into the wall behind him. Ron shot with a three-shot pattern. After the sixth round, Jack rose from his cover, fired two quick shots, and ducked again. There was no return fire. Just the sound of Ron crashing back into a pile of boxes. Jack peered over the table and saw Ron clutching his chest, blood spreading across his shirt.

"Enough!" Lacy shouted. "Enough."

Jack rose, saw the last remaining man standing in front of Lacy. He had his hands up, pistol aimed at the ceiling. Jack kept is aim trained on him.

"Reese," Jack said.

"Yeah?"

"Check on Danny."

Reese stepped out from cover and went to Danny. She kicked his 9mm away and began checking his wounds.

Just then, Ben burst into the room. Everyone flinched at the sight of him. And the man in front of Lacy, perhaps on instinct, fired a shot that hit Ben in the side. He staggered and fell to the ground.

"Ben!" Jack shouted. He fired at the last remaining guard. The guy fell, and the room fell into a tense silence, the only sound Ben and Danny's labored breathing.

Jack rushed to Ben's side. "Hang in there."

Ben nodded weakly. "I'll be fine. Just finish this."

With the immediate threat neutralized, Jack and Reese turned their attention to Lacy. She was trying to slip out the back door. Marcus was already across the room, pistol drawn and aimed at her.

"Stop, Lacy," Marcus said.

The door slipped off her fingertips and fell shut. For a moment, she stood with her back to them, shoulders slumped. Her exhale was forced and audible even amid Ben and Danny's ragged breaths. Lacy turned, slowly, drawing her shoulders back. A pistol hung from her right hand. By the time she faced them, she looked defiant. Her gaze swept the room, falling on Ron for a moment too long. A moment that said he was more than just her ex-husband who she ragged on incessantly any time he was around her. It was all a ruse, Jack figured, the way he treated her.

Marcus gestured for Lacy to come to him. She didn't move.

"It's over, Lacy," Marcus said.

"You don't understand." Lacy said. "It's not what it looks like."

"Save it," Jack said. "We know everything."

She stared at him for a moment and shook her head. "You have no idea what you're getting into."

Jack moved closer. "Then enlighten us. Who else is involved? And where's the evidence that proves it? 'Cause we already have everything we need on you."

Lacy smirked as her gaze darted toward Marcus. "You'll never take us all down. There's more at play here than you realize."

And that's when Jack heard it. One syllable. Spoken by the man who had wanted him dead for the better part of two decades.

"Now."

CHAPTER 35

"What have you done?" Jack's thoughts raced to Mia and Sean, the danger they were in, miles away in Costa Rica. Marcus had threatened their lives if Jack didn't comply, didn't help him achieve his goal.

Marcus's face twisted into a cold smile. "Just ensuring I have leverage." He raised his pistol and without hesitation shot Lacy in the shoulder. The gunshot echoed through the bar, and Lacy cried out, falling to the ground, clutching her wound.

"No!" Jack started to move but Marcus aimed his pistol at him, a smug grin on his face.

With his other hand, Marcus pressed send on his phone. "Now my men in Costa Rica are getting their orders. One wrong move from you, and your brother and daughter are dead."

Jack froze, his mind racing. He couldn't afford to call Marcus's bluff. "You don't have to do this, Marcus. Call them off."

Marcus shook his head. "You never understood, Jack. This is about control. And now, I have all the control. You're going to do whatever I want you to do."

Jack's desperation grew. He had to find a way to turn the situation around, to save Mia and Sean. He knew he had to take

Marcus out now. He waited for an opening. But before it could happen, the back door swung forward and a man entered. And two more men entered from the other end of the room. Marcus's men from outside.

Marcus relaxed his grip on his pistol and his phone, and the phone's screen was now in Jack's view. He saw what Marcus hadn't. The call had failed.

"Drop your weapons," one of the men shouted.

Jack glanced at Reese, who stood frozen, her gaze darting between Jack and Marcus. Jack nodded at her, and she slowly lowered her weapon.

Marcus's smirk widened as he watched Jack's reaction. "That's better. Now, we're going to have a little chat about how things are going to play out from here."

Jack gritted his teeth. "What do you want? I helped you with this. We're over."

"No, we're not," Marcus said. "You're going to help me consolidate power. With Hennessey's network under my control, we'll have a monopoly on every operation from here to the border. And you, Jack, you're going to ensure it happens smoothly. Otherwise, your family pays the price."

Jack's heart pounded in his chest. He couldn't let Marcus win, but he couldn't risk Mia and Sean's lives either. He needed to buy time, to find a way to turn the tables.

"All right." Jack tried to sound compliant. "I'll do what you want. Just call off your men in Costa Rica."

Marcus raised an eyebrow. "Do you think I'm stupid, Jack? You'll comply first, then I'll consider it."

Jack glanced around the room at the fallen bodies. Some dead. Other's hanging onto life. He settled on Reese, wishing he could communicate with her silently and coordinate a final attack. Her eyes shifted to the open door, then back to him. She repeated the gesture, then started lowering herself to the floor.

Jack turned his head toward Marcus again when he saw a flash from outside. A glint of light off something metallic. And then Tilley came into view, flanked by two other officers in riot gear.

As a man with a riot shield burst through the doorway, Jack dropped to the ground. Amid a round of gunfire, he crawled toward Reese, who was moving to the overturned table. With a burst, he reached her location and peered around the table to see what was happening.

He caught sight of Ben, on his knees, squeezing off a round and taking one in return. A fatal hit. Jack winced as the man fell forward, eyes open, staring in his direction.

One of the cops took a round and dropped. So did one of Marcus's men. Marcus had managed to retreat to a favorable position. The man aimed at Jack and fired, but he managed to duck his head in time.

Another of Marcus's men dropped, but before he did, he took out a second cop, leaving only Tilley. Marcus stepped out from his position and had the officer dead to rights. Jack had a bead on Marcus and squeezed the trigger, but it was too late. The man had fired and hit his target. Tilley was dead before he hit the ground.

Marcus wasn't so lucky. The bullet had entered his chest on the left. Enough damage to end his life.

After the exchange, Jack failed to notice Marcus's last remaining man had Jack in his sights. Reese called out and fired. Another round ripped through the air. Jack dove at the sound of Reese's voice, narrowly missed being hit. The other man wasn't so lucky as Reese's round took him out.

They surveyed the carnage. Reese went to Tilley and confirmed he was gone. Jack took his time approaching Marcus, aware that the man could have one last play.

"Jack," Reese said.

"What?" he said.

"Lacy escaped."

"She won't get far. She's too injured."

The backdoor hung slightly ajar. Reese kicked it open. Just beyond the opening, Lacy lay on the ground, struggling to breathe.

"Looks like she took another round," Reese said.

"See what you can do for her."

Jack approached Marcus, his eyes never leaving the man's face. Marcus lay on the ground, blood pooling around him, but his eyes were still sharp, full of defiance.

"You think this ends with me?" Marcus spat, coughing up blood. "There are others. You can't stop it."

Jack knelt beside him, his expression hard. "Who else, Marcus? Who's pulling the strings?"

Marcus chuckled weakly, his strength fading. "You'll never find out. You're just one man, Jack. One man against a machine."

Reese joined Jack, her eyes flicking to Marcus, then to the fallen bodies around them. "We need to end this."

Jack nodded, his jaw clenched. "You're right." He leaned closer to Marcus, his voice cold. "Where's the evidence, Marcus? Where's the proof that ties everything together?"

Marcus's eyes fluttered, the light in them dimming. "The bar... behind the bar... safe... code is... 1952." His voice trailed off, and with one last shuddering breath, he was gone.

Jack stood. "Reese, check the safe. We need that evidence."

Reese nodded and moved quickly behind the bar, finding the hidden safe. She returned moments later holding folders and a flash drive. "This is it. This is what we need."

"Take pictures of everything."

While she did, Jack pulled out his phone and placed a call.

A familiar voice answered. "Magnitude investigations."

"The hell?" Jack glanced at the phone to make sure he dialed the correct number. "Brandon?"

"Jack?"

"Yeah. What the hell kinda crap is Magnitude Investigations?"

"Just trying it on for size." Brandon laughed, but quickly stopped. "What's going on? Why are you calling so early? Or, maybe late, wherever you are."

"I need you to check on Mia and Sean."

"What's up?"

"They may be in danger. An old associate found me, maybe set this whole thing in Montana up to get me here somehow. I'm not sure. But he says he has men in Costa Rica. I need you to check on them, and I need you to get me from here to there."

"I'm going too," Reese said.

Jack stared at her for a moment. "No, I can't ask you to do that. This isn't your battle."

"It involves you, so it is. Plus, the feds will be here tomorrow and I'll be off to somewhere else."

"You reach out to me. I'll come back to wherever you are."

"You know they aren't going to let it be so easy this time."

"Make that travel plans for two," Jack said.

"I've got a helicopter that'll be ready to go in thirty. That'll get you to an airfield with a private jet to San Diego. From there, you'll have new docs and transport to Costa Rica."

"Great, thanks Brandon." Jack glanced down at Marcus's life-less body. "Also, going to text you a bunch of documents. I need you to get them in the hands of the right people. If they ask questions, ignore them. Everything they need should be there. And there's a thumb drive. Send instructions on how to get that to you."

They ended the call and Jack walked to Ben. He'd seen him take the round that ended his life. There was nothing he could have done. Ben was supposed to wait outside. If he had, he might've perished. Or perhaps he'd have managed to stop Marcus's men from entering. Jack let those thoughts fade. They weren't what happened.

His phone buzzed again. Brandon had sent the helicopter's location.

CHAPTER 36

Sitting in the medium jet Brandon had arranged for transport from San Diego to Costa Rica, Jack managed to still his mind. It might have been the first time in years he didn't have a single thought. The peace and tranquility were disturbed by his ringing phone. He glanced at the screen. Brandon.

"What's up, Mr. Magnitude?"

Brandon laughed. "Don't worry, we're not using that."

"You're really gonna go through with this, huh? You're own investigation agency."

"Why not? Look, we can talk about that later, including your role—"

"*My* role?"

"—but first let me update you." Brandon tapped on his keyboard. "Like I told you earlier, Sean and Mia are in a safe location. I was still worried that Marcus's connections—they aren't his men but he has some arrangement with these guys, though I doubt they'll care if he's dead—could reach them, so I pulled some strings and they're detained for at least a week. Should give you plenty of time to get in, find them, and get out. I wouldn't linger too long though. These guys will be pissed once they're on the street again. I'm still working on their specific connection with Marcus."

"Can't thank you enough."

"Don't go sucking me off yet, pal," Brandon said. "There may be more I don't know about. This is all going what I got off of Marcus's phone. You need to keep your guard up while down there. You might be walking into a hornet's nest. Plus, there is a gonna be a shitload of fallout from this up here. Montana. D.C. Multiple agencies. I'm gonna do my best to keep your name out of this, but the Feds are gonna realize Reese is gone. How long you think before they piece it all together?"

"Couple weeks to a couple months." Jack laughed. "The way things are run these days, I'll put my money on a couple of months."

Reese slipped into the seat across from Jack. She set two glasses of bourbon on the table, slid one across to Jack. He took a sip and let the warm liquid burn his throat.

"This is still serious, buddy," Brandon said.

"I won't relax until we are out of the country with Mia and Sean and his family. Speaking of, can you help with that?"

"That'll be easy. Get you out by boat, probably to South America for a bit, then back home."

"Home," Jack said. "Where the hell is that?"

"That's for you to figure out," Brandon said. "I gotta go."

Jack set his phone on the table. Reese reached across, took his hand in hers.

"How's the injuries?" Jack said.

She pulled up her sleeve and showed him the wrap on her arm. "They got me patched up. Gave me some antibiotics. Guess I'm gonna live. You okay with that?"

Jack shrugged. "I can keep you around for a while, I suppose."

She smiled, took a drink, leaned back. It had been years since they first met. More than a few years since Texas. Yet she looked the same. Youthful. Beautiful. But it was more than that. With her hand in his, he felt at peace.

"I overheard some of your call," she said.

"I'm aware," he said.

"No place to call home anymore?" she said.

Jack smiled. "I'm thinking it might just be wherever I am with you."

Join the L.T. Ryan reader family & receive a free copy of the Jack Noble prequel, *The First Deception* with bonus story, *The Recruit*. Click the link below to get started:

https://ltryan.com/jack-noble-newsletter-signup-1

ALSO BY L.T. RYAN

Find All of L.T. Ryan's Books on Amazon Today!

The Jack Noble Series

The Recruit (free)

The First Deception (Prequel 1)

Noble Beginnings

A Deadly Distance

Ripple Effect (Bear Logan)

Thin Line

Noble Intentions

When Dead in Greece

Noble Retribution

Noble Betrayal

Never Go Home

Beyond Betrayal (Clarissa Abbot)

Noble Judgment

Never Cry Mercy

Deadline

End Game

Noble Ultimatum

Noble Legend

Noble Revenge

Never Look Back (Coming Soon)

Bear Logan Series

Ripple Effect

Blowback

Take Down

Deep State

Bear & Mandy Logan Series

Close to Home

Under the Surface

The Last Stop

Over the Edge

Between the Lies (Coming Soon)

Rachel Hatch Series

Drift

Downburst

Fever Burn

Smoke Signal

Firewalk

Whitewater

Aftershock

Whirlwind

Tsunami

Fastrope

Sidewinder (Coming Soon)

Mitch Tanner Series

The Depth of Darkness

Into The Darkness

Deliver Us From Darkness

Cassie Quinn Series

Path of Bones

Whisper of Bones

Symphony of Bones

Etched in Shadow

Concealed in Shadow

Betrayed in Shadow

Born from Ashes

Blake Brier Series

Unmasked

Unleashed

Uncharted

Drawpoint

Contrail

Detachment

Clear

Quarry (Coming Soon)

Dalton Savage Series

Savage Grounds

Scorched Earth

Cold Sky

The Frost Killer (Coming Soon)

Maddie Castle Series

The Handler

Tracking Justice

Hunting Grounds (Coming Soon)

Affliction Z Series

Affliction Z: Patient Zero

Affliction Z: Abandoned Hope

Affliction Z: Descended in Blood

Affliction Z : Fractured Part 1

Affliction Z: Fractured Part 2 (Fall 2021)

Love Noble? Savage? Hatch? Maddie? Get your very own L.T. Ryan merchandise today! Click the link below to find coffee mugs, t-shirts, and even signed copies of your favorite L.T. Ryan thrillers! https://ltryan.ink/EvG_

ABOUT THE AUTHOR

L.T. RYAN is a *Wall Street Journal, USA Today,* and Amazon bestselling author of several mysteries and thrillers, including the *Wall Street Journal* bestselling Jack Noble and Rachel Hatch series. With over eight million books sold, when he's not penning his next adventure, L.T. enjoys traveling, hiking, riding his Peloton, and spending time with his wife, daughter and four dogs at their home in central Virginia.

* Sign up for his newsletter to hear the latest goings on and receive some free content ➜ https://ltryan.com/jack-noble-newsletter-signup-1
* Join LT's private readers' group ➜ https://www.facebook.com/groups/1727449564174357
* Follow on Instagram ➜ @ltryanauthor
* Visit the website ➜ https://ltryan.com
* Send an email ➜ contact@ltryan.com
* Find on Goodreads ➜ http://www.goodreads.com/author/show/6151659.L_T_Ryan

Printed in Great Britain
by Amazon

43553158R00126